A
Mediterranean
Affair

ANGELA AARON

D1403586

DEDICATION

For my dear camping friends,
this one's for you.
Italians may feed the world, but they also
inspire writers.

For Jules, thanks for the endless hours of
reading and rereading.
Your continued support is heartwarming
and forever appreciated.

ACKNOWLEDGMENTS

Cover Art by Fiona Jayde
http://fionajaydemedia.com

Editing by Bryl Tyne
http://bryltyne.com

Also Available from Angela Aaron

Sizzling romance at its barest
Mature- Sexually Explicit.

<u>Pleasure Island</u>

When Cassie Douglas unknowingly arrives at a sultry tropical island resort where the sole business is to provide the perfect pleasure fantasy, Cassie finds it difficult to overcome her inhibitions and join in the fun. When she meets the sexy resort owner, Cassie must decide what is real when it comes to matters of the heart.

Ryan MacKenna isn't about to let the feisty red-head disrupt his life or his business. He lives firmly by his set of self-imposed rules which keep business and pleasure very separate. However, from the first moment he meets Ms. Douglas, he is in danger of breaking every rule.

<u>The Fire of Beltane</u>

When Aedan is denied his soul mate that fateful Beltane night, he is given the gift of immortality, permitting him to wait for her prophesized return. Reunited after eleven-hundred years, he is disheartened to learn his true love holds no memory of him.

Wishing for a distraction from the winter doldrums, Aislinn never expects to be caught up in a whirlwind of magic and danger with a man she has spent her whole life dreaming about. What he asks of her tests the very reality she holds dear.

Now as Beltane approaches, and with time running out, Aedan and Aislinn must reach Ireland to pledge their love to one another. But in order to live out their destinies, they must overcome an ancient foe determined to see an end to their fated love.

Eleven hundred years he waited for her. He could lose her in a single moment.

Prologue

"What's the matter, Uncle?" Cupid inquired, darting in and out of the glistening pillars of the great golden palace, his light-colored curls bobbing as he flew. "Your usual reverie and celebrations not enough merriment for today?"

"Mind your impetuous tongue, Cupid. You know I am always concerned when I feel discontent among my protégés. He is of our very bloodline and I feel his unhappiness as if it were my own. No amount of libations will cure him of what ails him." Bacchus's dark coloring and surly mood strongly contrasted against two large columns he moved through, stepping out to the garden terrace overlooking the green fertile valleys of Mount Olympus. The view was a remarkable sight even on a troubling day such as this.

Cupid fluttered up alongside Bacchus, his feet hovering just inches above the ground.

"What is the matter with him?"

"He carries an empty heart. Love has forsaken him."

Cupid excitedly flew a circle around his uncle. "I can help with that."

"Do you not tire of meddling in the affairs of humans, Cupid?" Bacchus quipped suddenly disappearing and reappearing inside an opulently decorated great room. Bacchus commenced pacing, the marble floor cool under his bare feet. Cupid fluttered around anxiously, the breeze from his wings billowing the colorful tapestries that covered the ancient walls.

"You should mind your own business," Bacchus reprimanded.

"I do not meddle. I merely help out when help is needed," Cupid answered lowering himself to stand on the floor. He picked up several arrows resting on a hand carved wooden table and placed them in his quiver.

"This is what I do." Cupid explained as he straightened his mother's favorite 10,000-year-old vase. "Besides, my 'meddling', as you call it, helps make mother's job easier."

"Stop with arguing," Venus reprimanded, entering the room and hearing their conversation. "You both have a part to play in the great cosmos, but for heaven's sake, do not let Jupiter hear of your intervention in human lives. You know how he hates it when we manipulate the fates.

"Hypocrite," Bacchus mumbled under his breath.

Venus shot him a look.

"I don't involve the fates, Mother," Cupid assured.

"Good. You know how fickle they can be."

Cupid slipped the quiver over his shoulder, and then stretched his wings, testing them for the flight to earth.

"I see you are preparing for a trip? Where are you off to this time?" Venus asked, stepping over to her beloved son and straightening the quiver on his back.

You know I have the cruise ship business, mother. It's one of the ways I bring people together for me to work my magic.

"Is that how you are doing it? Clever. That's why I have been so busy lately," Venus noted.

"Hey, Unc... How about you get your guy to the ship and I'll take it from there."

"Do you think it...?"

"I think it is a splendid idea." Venus said looking at her half-brother. "Then you can stop brooding around my palace and get back to your business of drinking and festivity.

"He will be a difficult one," Bacchus warned.

"I'm sure I can take care of him," Cupid reassured, stretching his wings one final time before taking flight and circulating the great hall. "I'm up for a challenge." He called down from high above their heads. "I think I shall rather enjoy this." Cupid giggled at the prospect of planning another clandestine meeting

"Just be careful my dear," Venus called in warning as Cupid headed toward the exit.

"Always, Mother. You will know soon enough if all goes well."

<u>Chapter One</u>

Andrea removed the familiar looking envelope out of the stack of mail tossed on her desk by the office mail clerk as he hurriedly passed by. She knew exactly what the missive meant without even opening it. It meant Steve wasn't going to be home tonight as he'd promised. Big surprise. He never showed up when planned. She sighed, complacently. She'd grown accustomed to his nature over the years. His job often kept him moving from one place to the next. After five years with Steve, she was used to his frequent cancellations. Still the letdown, regardless how typical, wasn't any easier.

She opened the envelope, glancing inside.

"Another consolatory gift?"

Andrea pushed the thick auburn hair from her face and turned toward her cubical mate and close friend, Victoria. Andrea tried to mask the disappointment in her voice. "He's got another lead on an item he's been searching for."

"He always has another lead, Andi, and another and another—"

"That's his job."

"Why do you keep making excuses for him?"

"I'm not making excuses...."

Victoria shot a soured look Andrea's way.

"Okay, maybe I am," Andrea admitted. "But he means well."

"He might mean well, but when will you realize you are just another 'thing' to him. He collects 'things'."

Any other person making a comment like that would have angered Andrea, but she and Victoria's friendship extended back to middle school. They long ago gave up the pretense of polite conversation between them. Still, she knew her friend was right. Steve wasn't a bad person, just extremely immersed in his job to the point everything else in his life took a back seat, including her.

At first, her relationship with Steve seemed fine; she liked the freedom and spontaneity of having time to shop on a whim, or to pamper herself with a facial, or even to see a show she knew Steve had no interest in seeing. She often went out with girlfriends after work for "girls' night" at a local club. However, as the "girls' nights" became fewer and fewer, and her friends became involved in relationships, bought houses, settled down, thought about starting families, she realized she lived a mere dream of a life she'd never have. Steve was not apt to settle down. He was content to fly in, spend a few hours with her, and then fly out to his next appointment. Though she was sure his routine hadn't changed since day one, maybe she had, because she felt like she spent too much time alone these days.

"You've put your whole life on hold for a guy who's too busy to make your relationship a priority. He'd rather craft business deals than spend time with you."

"Why don't you tell me how you really feel, Vic?" Andrea quipped but silently asked herself why *was* she still with Steve?

Because being with Steve was comfortable, predictable, and familiar. It wasn't as if men were lined up, beating down her door to get to her.

"I'm not trying to hurt you, Andi. It's just you're a vibrant woman wasting the best years of your life waiting around for something that's not going to happen."

"But it could. One day."

"One day? When you're seventy? Come on...."

"I know. I know."

"Why do you continue to wait?"

"This time it's different." Andrea waved the envelope she held in her hand, avoiding her friend's question. "This is a ticket for a cruise. My dream cruise to Italy. He's going to finish up in California and then meet me in Naples for nine days of sun and fun in the Mediterranean. I think he's serious this time. He knows how much I've wanted to go to Italy." Andrea watched her friend roll her eyes.

"He's always serious but it never happens." Her friend shook her finger at her. "I know you, Andrea. You are not a kept woman bought with luxuries. Yet that's exactly how he treats you. This trip is just another in a long list of consolatory prizes."

Andrea chewed on her lip. Again, her friend was right. She had a whole houseful of gifts from Steve. Simple tokens to remind her of all the times he hadn't make their rendezvous.

"He must be serious about going. It's a cruise for couples. A romantic cruise. Why would he purchase these tickets if he didn't plan on going?" Still, she defended his intent.

"His assistant purchased the tickets," Victoria reminded with skepticism.

Andrea set the envelope on the laminate desk. "Doesn't matter who purchased the tickets. He's going. That's all that matters."

"Promise me one thing. If he doesn't show, that's it. Dump him. He may have good intentions, but his follow-throughs suck. It's not fair to you, Andi. He has strung you along far too long. It's time to move on and find someone who wants to be with you."

The electronic ring of the office phone provided Andrea the perfect excuse for not making any promises. Victoria turned to answer it.

Andrea spun around in her chair, ending the conversation. Despite her friend's concern and protests, as well as the nagging little voice of doubt that was a constant companion as of late, the promise of a fun filled, romantic vacation with Steve gave her hope. Perhaps he reevaluated how she fits into his life. Perhaps he finally realized what she meant to him. Maybe he planned on proposing. She smiled as she found her anticipation rising. Victoria was wrong this time, and Andrea would love the prospect of telling her friend just that, after the cruise.

Chapter Two

Andrea stood amidst the crowd on the pier gazing at the ship looming before her. The mighty vessel proved to be as equally intimidating and as magnificent as Mt. Vesuvius standing tall and majestic in the distance behind her. She'd never been on a cruise before, and although she knew the ships were big, it hadn't registered exactly how big until this precise moment as she stood, dwarfed by its enormous size.

Up ahead, over the throngs of people, she could see the ship's crew greeting the new passengers as they boarded the ship. It would be a few minutes before the crowd thinned allowing her to move forward. She took this moment to scan the sea of faces hoping to catch Steve. They had just spoken the night before and agreed that since they were arriving on different flights, meeting in the cabin on the ship would be easiest. The arrangement made perfect sense to her, considering the amount of passengers all trying to board at the same time.

This was a popular cruise on Cupid Cruise Lines. A couple's cruise. A romantic and enchanting journey through the Mediterranean: Italy, France, Spain. All the places she dreamed of one day visiting. She smiled to herself. This vacation would signal a new chapter in her and Steve's relationship. She didn't realize Steve was such a romantic. It was a nice change from his usual all-business demeanor. Maybe he really had changed. She was lucky she hadn't promised Victoria she would break it off with him.

She often asked herself why she hadn't gotten rid of him after the first year and his constant cancellations, but the truth was, she liked Steve and hoped he would come around when it came to their relationship. It looked like he might finally be changing. As she glanced at the envelope in her hand, relief washed over her.

Even with her attraction to Steve, Andrea knew if he continued to disregard their relationship she couldn't stay no matter how she felt about him. Now, thank goodness, she wouldn't have to go down heartbreak road. She smiled to herself, sighing, glancing at the couples around her. Yep, this promised to be the trip of a lifetime.

Andrea finally reached the ship's entrance, stepping up to the young man with a tablet who just finished with the couple before her.

"Good day, cara." The young man greeted, flashing a wide smile. He had such a sweet cherub looking face, blond curls bobbing as he spoke with a beautiful Italian accent.

"Mr....?" Andrea searched his shirt for a name tag. "Ah, Mr. Cupido." Andrea looked up smiling at his name, assuming it was part of the cruise's ambiance. After all it was Cupid Cruise Lines. "Mr. Cupido, I'm Andrea McDonald. My partner, Steve Robinson and I will be joining this cruise. Has he checked in by any chance?" Andrea watched as the young man made several taps on his tablet, and then looked up at her.

"Not yet, but there is still time, cara."

"He took a different flight."

"Ah, well perhaps he is on his way. Traffic this time of day is very busy. I will make note that he is on his way." The young man tapped a few words into his tablet.

Andrea offered the necessary paperwork and both tickets to the young man.

"You have one of our balconied cabins.

Superb choice. Your luggage has already arrived. You should find it in your room waiting for you. I think you and signore will find the accommodations to your liking and the views spectacular. I shall hold Signore Robinson's ticket for him." Mr. Cupido took one of the tickets and handed a packet to Andrea as he returned her paperwork, flashing another of his youthful smiles.

"Everything you need is in there." He touched the envelope. "If you go in that direction to the elevators, you can follow the signs to your suite."

"Thank you."

"My pleasure, cara. Enjoy your stay."

Andrea couldn't help chuckle at the little mischievous wink he gave as he pointed in the direction she was to go. He was adorable, she thought, too young of course, but cute just the same. She headed toward the elevator.

* * *

Lorenzo slammed the car door with too much gusto. He had better things to do than deliver gifts to some spoiled Yank, even if the gifts were the best bottles of vino produced at his winery. His job was the vineyard and the grapes, not playing delivery boy to spoiled cruise ship passengers.

Despite his displeasure at the prospect of driving all the way into town and to the crowded docks, Lorenzo couldn't turn down his grandfather when asked to make the delivery. He'd seemed rather distraught at the message he brought with the wine and had asked Lorenzo to pick up a bouquet of flowers to accompany the delivery. Though he hadn't revealed the details of the message inside the envelope, Lorenzo guessed it wasn't good.

"Just perfect." Lorenzo mumbled under his breath, spying the volume of passengers he would have to wade through to reach the ship. Letting out a huff, and tucking his hair behind his ears, he trudged forward into the crowd, weaving his way in and out and around until finally reaching someone who could help him. In his haste, however, he nearly knocked over the crewmember as he approached. It was the quick action of a man who dodged out of the way that prevented a collision.

"My apologies, signore, but I have a delivery for one of your passengers." Lorenzo held up the bottles of wine he juggled and waited for directions to the delivery area. The young crewmember looked at him curiously for a moment before an impish smile graced his boyish face.

"And what passenger are you here to see?" he inquired, rather hastily, scanning the sea of remaining passengers who needed to board.

Lorenzo shifted the bottles of wine into one arm and dug into his pocket. He pulled out a slip of paper. "Signorina Andrea McDonald. An American."

Half expecting to have the wine and flowers taken from him, Lorenzo was shocked when the man instead referred to his tablet, jotted something on his clipboard, took papers out of his pocket, and handed them to him.

"Well, Mr. Robinson, your lovely lady has already boarded."

Lorenzo looked at the number on the paper.

"It is your cabin number and ticket stub."

"But I thought.... Wait.... I'm not.... Don't I just give this to someone who will see she gets it?" Even Lorenzo knew he couldn't just wander about the ship.

"Just go to the left over there and look for the elevators. I'm sure Signorina McDonald will be very glad you have arrived and pleased with your gift."

"Wait. This isn't my gift...." Lorenzo's protest went unnoticed by the young crewmember who turned his attention to another person. Lorenzo threw a glance to the heavens then scanned the number on the papers before stuffing them in his pants pocket and heading in the direction the crewman had instructed him to go.

"This is ridiculous." Lorenzo grumbled, rounding one final corner, halting in front of a door with the same numbers as on the papers given him. He sighed, shifted his packages, and knocked on the door. He waited, tapping his foot impatiently. After a moment, he knocked again.

"It's open," called a female voice from the other side.

Bena. He thought *Good*. He was anxious to finish this task. Lorenzo turned the handle, pushed the door open with his toe, and stepped inside,

Much to his astonishment, sprawled out before him on the bed, wearing nothing more than the skimpiest lingerie, was a beautiful auburn haired woman, posed very provocatively.

"Oh merda!"

His eyes raked over the luscious vision an instant before decorum had him spinning around, turning his back to her, but not before noting her long legs and ample breasts that were barely contained by the silky material. *Bella donna*.

"Oh!" came the woman's surprised squeal. "Oh no. I'm so sorry."

Lorenzo could hear fabric rustling and assumed she'd covered herself. He glanced over his shoulder unable to resist one final look, smiling to himself at all that lovely flesh hastily concealed by a thick terry robe.

"I'm so sorry. I thought you were someone else. I expected...."

She was flustered, blushing and extremely embarrassed, judging by the red stain on her cheeks.

"Oh never mind," she mumbled.

Lorenzo cleared his throat. "I have a delivery for you." He lifted the bottles of wine and flowers and held them out for her.

"For me?" She took the bottles from him, still wearing the blush from her indiscretion. "Oh, my favorite wine." She giggled setting the bottles on a nearby table. "And are the flowers for me, also?"

"Si." He held out the bouquet.

Lorenzo watched as she held them up to her nose and inhaled, smiling at the aroma. While she fished in the bouquet for the card, Lorenzo turned to make his exit. That was, until he heard the wine bottles crashing to the floor. He spun around, finding she had swept them off the table. Her expression revealed her anger and what he recognized as dejection. He turned again ready to make a hasty exit when he heard her speak.

"He's not coming. My dream trip to the Mediterranean and I'm on the cruise alone." The woman flung the card and envelope to the floor.

Lorenzo watched as tears brimmed in her eyes and spilled over her cheeks as she sank down on the edge of the bed. Utter despair now replaced the sexy, sultry, playful look that only a moment ago graced her sweet face.

Time to get out of here, he thought, reaching for the doorknob and jerking open the door, not attempting to hide his apprehension. This was exactly why he didn't like to make deliveries. He didn't have any inclination to involve himself in other people's drama. He'd had enough of his own not that long ago and wanted to avoid anything remotely similar for a very long time.

Against what every instinct told him, he halted when she called out to him, and despite his best intension not to, he turned toward her. She wiped at her eyes and haphazardly reached for her purse. The sadness on her face undid him. His chest tightened then, as a flood of memories assaulted him. In his unexpected disarming, he realized she thought she had to tip him.

"No. Bella." Before she even looked up, he fled from the room.

Chapter Three

Lorenzo dragged his weary body to the large rustic kitchen, poured himself a cup of coffee, and slumped down into a chair at the large planked table across from his grandfather.

"Good morning," Lorenzo's grandfather greeted. "You are up earlier than ever."

"Buon giorno, Nonno." Although his grandfather spoke perfect English, Lorenzo liked to use the old tongue out of respect for the man who'd raised him.

"I think your greeting belies your true state this morning." His grandfather was more than observant.

"I didn't sleep well last night." Well, that was an understatement. He hadn't slept at all. Not one wink. The distraught expression on the American woman's face haunted him every time he tried to close his eyes. Her misery only served to rekindle old wounds he tried so hard to keep suppressed.

"Does this have anything to do with the delivery I asked you to make yesterday?"

"Nonno, you know very well it has everything to do with that. You knew what that note said."

"I thought you'd be sympathetic; show some compassion and maybe a kind word or two for her."

"You know very well I don't talk about it."

"You need to talk about what happened. You need to get over it and start living again."

"Yes, well. I didn't stick around for a conversation."

"No? She was attractive, no?"

Lorenzo recalled the image of her sprawled out so seductively on the bed. Attractive wasn't even close to the erotic image she presented him.

"She was very attractive."

"And you didn't talk to her?"

"Enough." Lorenzo stood abruptly. "Look, Nonno, I appreciate your attempt at match-making or therapy or whatever you're doing, but I'm not interested."

"If you are not interested, then you would be more rested this morning."

Damn the perception of the old man. He was spot on with the cause of Lorenzo's restlessness this morning. Seeing Signorina McDonald left alone dredged up old wounds he had pushed aside long ago.

"Okay, so her plight did tug at me."

"She probably could use a friend right now, and Lord knows you need a friend as well. Seize the opportunity, Lorenzo. Stop letting life pass you by. I remember a boy who was always up for an adventure with a lovely lady."

Lorenzo did recall Ms. McDonald saying she would be alone now on her dream cruise. What a dream this turned out to be for her. He knew all about ruined dreams. Okay, he had to stop thinking about this. It made him crazy. He had chores to do and she was well out of port by now. Lorenzo set his coffee cup in the sink before pausing to kiss his grandfather on the head.

"I appreciate your concern, but I'm all right, Nonno, and I've had enough adventures."

"You're too young to be alone."

"And you're a hopeless romantic, Nonno. I'll be out in the fields."

Lorenzo exited the kitchen and on the veranda that circled the old home stood, silently surveying the rows of cultivated vines in the distance as far as his eye could see. His grandfather was still a foolish dreamer. He never stopped believing in coincidences and hunches. There had been a time not too long ago Lorenzo himself would have enjoyed a carefree adventure just for the fun of it, but one giant heartbreak left him tainted and not so interested in chasing dreams.

Yet, the sad face of Ms. McDonald seemed burned into his psyche and a constant tug on his heart since yesterday. Why should he care about her? Thousands of people every day lost loves. He and Ms. McDonald were just two more in the great succession of broken hearted. Still, her words "this was my dream vacation" echoed in his brain. Her only memory of his beautiful country would be a kiss-off note and wilted flowers. Didn't seem fair.

This was ridiculous, he reminded himself. He didn't even know her. Still, what he saw of her, and that was actually quite a bit, intrigued him. He smiled thinking of her laid before him like an offering. Definitely spirited, he admitted, and tempting for sure with her long auburn hair and crystal blue eyes. She could make a man rethink chasing dreams. He'd spent half the night fighting a hard-on just thinking about her sprawled on the bed ready for sex.

Lorenzo's grandfather came out the side

door and stood alongside him, also staring out over the fields. Wordlessly he slipped a piece of paper into Lorenzo's palm.

Lorenzo looked at him in question.

"The cruise lines scheduled ports," he stated. "If you hurry you may reach her in Livorno."

Lorenzo saw the slight hint of a twinkle in his grandfather's eye.

"You are a dreamer, Nonno."

"So I've been told."

Andrea tossed the brochures on the bed. She no longer held any interest in an excursion to Pisa or to Florence. Frankly, she just wanted to go home. Victoria had been right. Steve would always put his job before her. Damn, if this trip wasn't just another excuse-filled gift. She would truly never mean anything more to him than a soft body and possibly a softer heart to fall back on if and when he needed as much. Andrea wasn't even sure he needed that anymore... or maybe he had someone else she knew nothing about. Despite the anger welling up inside her, tears formed at the corners of her eyes. Damn him.

Victoria's persistent nagging about Steve finally sank in. Andrea had decisions to make concerning him.

She stepped out to the balcony and looked

over the rail. She saw the hustle and bustle of the port to her right, noticed the wide open ocean to her left, and felt the big empty space in her heart. Tears spilled from her eyes and ran down her cheeks. She didn't even bother to wipe them away. How she wished she had the bottles of wine she hastily smashed yesterday. She could use a drink, despite being morning— anything to numb the emptiness that gnawed at her gut.

A knock on the cabin door interrupted Andrea's musings. She figured it was housekeeping or whatever they called it on the ship. So she stepped inside, swiping haphazardly at the tears on her face before reaching for the door.

Much to her surprise, it wasn't the cleaning crew standing in the hallway outside her door; it was the man who delivered the wine and flowers yesterday.

Six foot plus of dark Italian male filled the doorway. His broad shoulders and muscled arms nearly spanned the width of the entrance. His deep black hair was pulled back into a ponytail, accentuating the chiseled lines of his strong jaw and well-defined cheekbones. His eyes were dark as they studied her.

"Buon giorno, Signorina McDonald."

Andrea wiped the remainder of her tears

from her face.

"Buon giorno," she answered, skeptically eyeing the two bottles of wine in the man's arms. Had she not just wished for a drink of wine? That was weird.

The man boldly stepped in, raking his eyes over her from head to foot. "I see you do not expect anyone today." Andrea felt the blush burst across her cheeks, instantly recognizing he spoke of the fact she was dressed and not half-naked on the bed.

"Ya, well. I won't be expecting him ever again. And if those bottles of wine are from him, you can just take them back out with you."

"Nay, Signorina. I heard you say they were your favorite. It's a shame you didn't get to taste any yesterday—so I brought you more. A better year, if I do say so."

Andrea eyed him quizzically. "Did Steve put you up to this?"

"Steve? No. The last bottles didn't come with good news. Your dream vacation shouldn't start out wrong. I didn't want you to leave my beautiful country filled with bad memories nor without tasting the best vino produced in Italy."

Andrea couldn't help a slight smile at this boast and the fact he remembered her saying this was her dream vacation. She was half-tempted to open the bottles this very moment and share a drink with the man.

"Then, thank you." She offered as he turned to place the bottles of wine on the small table. "By the way, how do you keep getting on the ship? Aren't their rules about this sort of thing?"

"Si. It's strange. I keep running into the same crewman who insists I am your traveling companion, Steven Robinson." He tapped his chest shirt pocket where the edges of folded papers showed. "He is young and maybe inexperienced. Each time I've come, I've tried to explain that I'm not Signor Robinson but he is so busy he just waves me by."

"Oh," Andrea answered. She should talk to the ship's crewman and straighten this out in case Steve did decide to join her.

She watched him snatch up the brochures she had tossed aside on the bed earlier, and scan each one.

"Ah... Florence. The tourist center of the country," he said.

"I have reservations at the Uffizi Gallery. The travel agency told me to book early if I wanted to see it. I guess it's crowded."

"Si. It's very crowded."

"But now...." She sighed, resigned her desire to see a Botticelli would have to wait for another time. "I will miss seeing Botticelli."

"I'll take you there," he said suddenly, turning back toward her.

Andrea's gaze snapped to him, taken aback by his impromptu offer. "No. It's okay."

"Si? You and I will go."

"No. It's all right, really. Besides the cruise bus already left."

"I can take you. In my auto. What time are your reservations?"

"One."

Andrea watched him check his watch. "We can make it if we hurry."

"I can't. Honestly, you don't have to—"

"Nonsense. You must see what you wanted to see. Hurry. We need to go."

"Oh. But I can't just... I don't even know you."

"My name is Lorenzo Caggiano. Same as the wine on that table." He pointed to the bottles he had brought. "My great uncle started Caggiano wines. My grandfather and I live and work on the estate with the rest of the family."

"No wonder you brag about your wine."

"I do not brag. It is the best."

Andrea found herself laughing at his confident Italian manner. "Oh."

"Si. I'll tell you more on the way."

Andrea found his enthusiasm infectious if

not entertaining. His smile seemed sincere, tugging at the corners of his dark eyes. How could she not find him charming? He had quite a sense of adventure, she noted, especially after bringing the wine up to Livorno for her. An afternoon at the Uffizi sure beat sitting alone in her cabin. In the very least, she would get to see the Botticelli paintings; at best, she would spend the afternoon with a very attractive man.

"Sure. Why not," Andrea agreed, grabbing her sweater, her spontaneity surprising even her. She stuffed the tickets and her cruise passes into her purse. "Do you think it possible to visit the Academia Gallery to see 'David' or the Medici Museum?" Andrea asked suddenly excited to be on her way to Florence.

Lorenzo laughed. "Typical tourist," he said amusedly. "That is a lot, but I will do my best to show you all Florence has to offer before you must return to the ship."

* * *

Florence was about an hour and a half from the docks but Lorenzo was sure they covered the distance in half that time. He expertly maneuvered his blue Audi Cabriolet convertible through the busy traffic that more than once had Andrea white-knuckle gripping her seat, when she wasn't trying to keep her hair out of her eyes.

Ah, he probably should have warned her about the car being a convertible, but then her smile told him she wasn't minding too much. Every now and then, she'd look over at him, with lower lip tucked under her teeth then burst into a full-fledged grin. He found her smile so enchanting and genuine; he couldn't help himself from grinning back. Damn, but he actually felt carefree. This surprised the hell out of him. He was sure that sensation had abandoned him long ago.

Speaking over the din of the open car was nearly impossible, but when he saw something of interest along the route, he slowed down to point it out to her, leaning over to explain what it was. He could tell she appreciated his thoughtfulness and he found this refreshing. Maybe this would turn out to be a great day after all, as his grandfather had predicted.

Getting around Florence was usually a traffic nightmare, but having lived there for a time, Lorenzo was familiar with some of the less traveled ways around the busy city. It didn't take him long to find a place to park the car that would be central to where Andrea wanted to visit.

First on their agenda was the Uffizi

Gallery. Being one of the oldest and most famous of the Western world meant it was also the busiest. The museum split their tours into smaller tours to allow more people to see works that are more specific.

Andrea held tickets for the paintings in the Halls of the Masters, which meant there might be time to visit the other places in the city she wanted to see. He was determined that she at least see "David." Everyone must see *that* statue while in Florence.

Lorenzo loved watching her face as she strolled from one painting to the next, *oohing* and *aahing* at each one. Giotto, Fabriano, Veneziano, Lippi, Raphael, she studied the details of every canvas. An early work of Da Vinci as well as a rare painting by Michelangelo especially moved her. She sighed with astonishment when she spied a Titian and Caravaggio, but it was Botticelli that captivated her attention. "Primavera" and "Birth of Venus" are what she had come to see, and she stood gazing at these paintings with such absolute awe that her affection for these works moved him.

"I have loved the painting "The Birth of Venus" my entire life. You have no idea what it means to me to be standing here looking at it in person. Thank you so much for bringing me here." Andrea looked over at him then, and he actually became choked up to see the unshed tears in her eyes. She was truly moved, not only by seeing the paintings, but also from his kindness in making a dream of hers a reality.

So touched by her open display of honesty, any words Lorenzo intended to speak to her caught in his throat. He just reached over and gave her hand a quick squeeze, acknowledging her appreciation before stepping away to allow her time with the paintings.

This kind of openness from a woman was foreign to him. Come to think of it, he had never seen such an honest display of emotions from his.... Well... he wasn't going to tread those waters again. Regardless, such truth was refreshing to see. He had convinced himself it didn't exist, and yet here right in front of him with an almost stranger so choked up by the simple gesture of gazing on a painting, it rendered him speechless.

After a few moments and after he found his voice, Lorenzo leaned over and whispered, "Take your time. I'll be back in a few moments."

When he returned a short while later, he watched Andrea study the painting as if committing to memory every last detail and soaking in every nuance of the experience before she finally turned to him. She took a deep breath. "We can go now."

"Are you sure? You may want a few more minutes."

"No. I'm good. I am so pleased to have seen these paintings in person. Grazie, Lorenzo."

Lorenzo appreciated she used his language to thank him. "Prego, cara. I am glad I was able to make it happen. Now I have an idea. How about a quick lunch and a gelato before we make our way to find 'David'?"

"I'd like that."

"I know a quaint little place not too far that serves the best sandwiches," Lorenzo suggested.

"Perfecto."

Lorenzo couldn't help but laugh at her attempt to say "perfect". "Not quite. It's 'Perfetto'"

"Oh. I'm sorry. Perfetto, then."

"Perfetto." Lorenzo took her hand, leading her out of the museum.

* * *

Once seated at the quaint outdoor café, Andrea felt like she finally had a second to catch her breath. The last few hours were busy for sure. It was nice to have a moment to relax and people watch.

Florence was teeming with a diversity of people from so many cultures, yet none was as intriguing as the man sitting before her ordering them a porchetta and mozzarella sandwich in Italian.

Flashing a smile in between sentences, she had no idea what he said except for the type of food he was ordering. Nonetheless, he carried on quite an animated conversation with the waiter. When he finally produced a business card from his pocket and handed it to the waiter, Andrea figured the conversation had been about his wine business.

What a surprise she held that morning when she opened her door and found Lorenzo standing there. Who knew he was one of the owners of the vineyard that produced her favorite wine and that he took enough pride in his wine to bring her two more bottles. Never in a million years had she expected anything like that, nor to be running all over Florence with him now. This day had certainly taken a turn for the better.

He was wonderful company, pleasant, funny, and even respectful of her need to see the arts. Steve would have never been that patient to give her a few moments to soak in the whole experience—but Lorenzo had. This man intrigued her.

She noticed the waiter turning to leave, and Lorenzo's attention returning to her.

"Perdonami. Forgive my manners. I merely pointed out his wine selection could be better and we had a wonderful modest line that would go well with his menu."

Andrea just laughed. "Ever the salesman."

"Never hurts to advertise." Lorenzo shifted in his seat, gesturing to the buildings around him. "Florence is magnifico, no?"

"Spectacular. I love that we're sitting right in the middle of all these ancient buildings and sculptures. It is an incredible city, vibrant and alive. It's a great place to visit, but I think this would be too busy a place for me to live."

"Even with all the art?"

"Yes, even then."

"Well, cara, I have to agree with you. This city moves much too fast for me. Things are much slower at the vineyard."

"Things are much slower where I'm from, too."

"And where are you from?" Lorenzo turned his full attention on her as he waited for her to answer. Andrea felt disconcerted he was so attentive. It was not so most of the time with Steve, with a phone in one hand, trying to talk to both her and a client at the same time.

"Chicago."

"Well that is a big city." Lorenzo stated.

"I know. I don't actually live in Chicago. I just work there. I live about fifteen miles north of the city in a small town. I keep a small apartment with a beautiful view of Lake Michigan. I totally lucked out with finding such a place. Found it through a co-worker. A nice old lady wanted to rent out the upper part of her old home."

"Ah." Lorenzo nodded. "And what do you do in Chicago?"

"Mostly dream of coming to Italy."

Lorenzo broke out in a laugh. "Okay, he chuckled. When you are not dreaming of visiting Italy. What do you do?"

"I am a legal assistant at a law firm that specializes in environmental cases."

"That sounds interesting."

"It is. It's mostly paper pushing and filing documents at the courthouse, but it allows me to meet interesting people and keeps me busy. I work with a dear friend, so we have a lot of fun."

"Is that how you met the man you were supposed to be with today?"

"No. I met him at a restaurant; we literally bumped into one another."

Andrea recalled the accidental meeting. Steve had been so apologetic that he'd caused her to spill wine on her dress, after bumping into her while talking on his phone. His sweet smile instantly captivated her. She spent the rest of the night allowing him to fuss over her, buy her dinner and getting to know him. The next day an envelope arrived for her at her office. In it were gift cards to some of the finest department stores along with a note from Steve apologizing once again for ruining her dress and an invitation to dine with him again.

"He made me spill my wine and bought me dinner. The rest, you could say is history."

"But, he is not here."

"No. Steve's job keeps him extremely busy." Andrea did not want to go into the sordid details of how many other times he had stood her up or how empty life was more often than not with Steve as a boyfriend, while sitting here, in the heart of Florence, with such a delightful, thoughtful man as Lorenzo.

She was grateful that at that precise moment the waiter brought their food, halting any further conversation about Steve.

The plate of food placed before her had her mouth watering before ever taking a bite. Braised pork slices topped with mozzarella, green peppers, and onions all piled high on an

Italian bun.

"You look at your sandwich as you looked at the Botticelli," Lorenzo said, taking a bite of his lunch but watching her.

Andrea laughed. "It looks delicious."

"You won't know how delicious unless you eat it."

Andrea didn't hesitate any longer and dug into the tempting fare before her.

"Wow," she said after several bites. "They don't make them like this at home."

"There are places that do," Lorenzo corrected.

"Maybe it tastes better because I'm in Italy."

"Perhaps," he agreed.

"Lorenzo, have you been to the states?"

"Uh-huh." He nodded, swallowing his bite, washing it down with bottled water before he continued. "I attended Boston University. I spent a lot of time in New York. And there are some great Italian restaurants in New York."

"That is why you speak such good English."

"Yes. I planned to stay in the states after school, but I had a change of plans and I came back to Italy, instead.

"What changed?"

Andrea noticed Lorenzo hesitated before

answering her.

"I was needed at the family vineyard."

"Well I can't blame you for wanting to come home. I'll bet the vineyard is beautiful. The Italian countryside is breathtaking. What a wonderful place to live."

"Ah...." Lorenzo sat up, changing the subject. "I have something for you." He fished in his pockets retrieving a small item he kept hid in his fist.

"Hold out your hand." Andrea held out her hand, palm up, biting her lip in anticipation of what he could possibly have for her.

"It's nothing really, just something to remember your Botticelli."

Lorenzo dropped a keychain in her hand that sported a plastic replica of both of her favorite paintings. The kind gesture caught her totally off guard.

"Oh my. This is so kind of you, Lorenzo. I can't believe you did this."

"It was nothing, bella; just a small token to remember your trip."

She closed her hand around it, affectionately. "I will treasure this. Thank you, Lorenzo."

Andrea couldn't help but return his smile. He was genuinely pleased she liked his gift. This was a day to put in the memory books. A total stranger had done more for her in just a few hours than Steve had done in the five years she had dated him. She couldn't help feel a bit of fondness toward Lorenzo.

"Let's finish our lunch and find *Signor David*, no?"

"Let's."

* * *

For the third time that day, this lovely American woman had Lorenzo choked up beyond words. The first was as he'd watched her look at her paintings. The second, when she so gratefully accepted the keychain he'd given her over lunch, deeply moved by the simple token. The third time was at this very moment as she stood, looking up at Michelangelo's "David." He could see in her eyes and by her expression her awe in the magnificent sculpture. She made him feel proud to be Italian and have some connection to the artist.

It intrigued him by how easily her emotions played across her face. Lorenzo found it so refreshing he couldn't help gaze at her for long moments. What a difference from another woman he used to know. One he thought, at the time, he knew so well.

Andrea was so easy to talk to, to be with,

he found he almost opened up over lunch and poured out all the miserable details of being abandoned at the alter when she had asked him why he left America. Thank God, the waiter had brought their food at that precise moment and kept him from making a fool of himself. How easily the wretched memory of standing before a sea of confused faces announcing there would be no wedding came back to him. Now, after all this time, he found he wanted to speak of the gut-twisting despair at suddenly losing everything He attributed this desire to the fact he felt so damn at ease with this woman; it disarmed him. He was beside himself, finding he wanted to tell all of his past to a stranger. What had gotten into him? It took him several moments to shake the feelings and remind himself this was only a casual day with a new friend.

Still, he had to admit, he hadn't had this much fun nor felt this lighthearted in a long time. He thoroughly enjoyed her company.

"Hand me your phone and let me take a photo of you with the statue."

Andrea obliged. He even took several with his phone, and when another tourist offered to take their photo together, he didn't think twice before jumping into the picture with her.

Lorenzo checked his watch. They had to

leave no later than five o'clock to return to the ship in time for departure. Still, he was determined she would see all she'd asked to see. He would make this the best day for her, something she would remember always.

"If you want a quick look at the Medici chapels, we must say 'arrivederci' to David and be on our way."

"The Medici museum is several blocks from here. We'll have to hurry." Lorenzo grabbed her hand and broke into a sprint, tugging her along, laughing at the way they dodged in and out of the crowds of people in their attempt to reach their destination.

When they reached the museum, both stopped only long enough to catch their breaths before going inside chapels.

"Oh my," was Andrea's reaction to the marbled tombs and ornate rooms before her. "This is unbelievable. Spectacular. Opulent."

"It is truly magnifico, no?"

"Yes." Andrea sighed. "I'm just blown away by Michelangelo's work. It is so hard to comprehend one person could have so much talent, and one family so wealthy."

"Take your photos, bella. Unfortunately for us, time grows short."

Lorenzo watched, as Andrea made sure she got a photo of every tomb, of every room and statue, before taking her phone and snapping photos of her in front of the marble tombs. Once again, another patron offered to take their picture together in front of "Madonna and Child." Lorenzo gathered her up in his arms and held her in front of him. He bent down and placed his face next to hers, secretly enjoying the close contact.

"Fitting don't you think, that you are Lorenzo and our photo is in front of Lorenzo's tomb?" Andrea asked, stepping away, taking back her camera.

"Perhaps it was meant to be," Lorenzo answered, checking his watch again.

"I hate to be a clock watcher, bella, but we must start back to the car."

Lorenzo didn't see disappointment on her face, only gratitude. This surprised him. However, what surprised him even more was suddenly and without warning, she threw her arms around him, hugging him and thanking him for all the wonderful things he'd showed her today. He instinctively placed his arms around her, noting how good she felt in them. Unfortunately, propriety dictated the moment and he released her and stepped away.

"Prego, bella. It was my pleasure."

Lorenzo took her hand as they strolled to his car, pointing out other noteworthy buildings, cathedrals, and statues as they walked.

The drive back to the ship was more subdued than the previous trip. Lorenzo had to keep reminding himself to keep the correct speed, as he found he wanted to slow down to make every minute last as long as it could. He didn't want the trip and their time together to end. He hadn't had this much fun in such a long time and he wanted it to last. He noticed Andrea was much quieter; also, soaking in the details of the countryside as they drove, flashing him her appreciative smile every now and again.

He'd like to think she too felt melancholy about their day ending, but realistically supposed she was only weary from such a busy day.

As he pulled into a parking lot near the ports, Lorenzo thought he noticed a look of regret cross her face as she glanced at the ship in the distance. Perhaps he only imagined it for she was all smiles as he held the car door for her and she stepped out onto the cement.

"I will walk you to the ship."

"Oh, Lorenzo, you don't need to go to such trouble. You've been so kind already. I have a few extra moments, and I think I will check out a few vendors on my way to the dock."

She turned to him. Standing before him, she took his hands. "I've had the most wonderful day possible. I can't thank you enough for everything you did for me. You were so gracious to offer me the chance to visit Florence. I will never forget."

"Si. I too enjoyed our day and am glad I was able to brighten your trip."

Lorenzo bent and kissed her left cheek and then her right, in the traditional manner of his country. She squeezed his hands before letting go.

"Arrivederci." Andrea waved as she stepped away.

"Arrivederci," Lorenzo called back as he watched her disappear into the crowd.

Chapter Four

Andrea looked out over the balcony and sighed. A beautiful sight greeted her this morning, but once again, the feeling of loneliness settled over her. The sun had risen over the ocean. The ship docked overnight night in the Ville Franche. The best of what the French Riviera had to offer just footsteps away. Palm trees, blue seas, wonderful beaches awaited her, yet she felt rather half-hearted about the prospect of spending the day alone.

The previous day had been so much fun, Lorenzo had been such wonderful company, it would be hard to top that. She viewed the photos on her phone repeatedly all evening, not wanting the special way she felt to fade.

She was amazed at the instant connection she shared with Lorenzo. She was so comfortable around him and him around her, noting how he held her hand and kissed her as if he'd known her forever. Maybe it was his suave Italian manner or the way he made her laugh.

Whatever it was, she missed him. They'd hit it off so well. When it was time to return, she found she was sad. As they reached the ship's port, she could only manage a hasty good-bye so he wouldn't see the tears forming in her eyes. She looked down at the keychain in her hand. Such a simple gift and yet it meant more to her than anything Steve had ever bought for her. She had to admit, Lorenzo's thoughtfulness touched a deep place inside her. A place Steve had never been. She appreciated Lorenzo opening her eyes to what Steve was not.

Andrea decided she would leave the ship for a while and wander around with the other tourists. Perhaps it would help take her mind off the unexpected emptiness she harbored. Perhaps she could find some gift for Victoria in the numerous shops that lined the ocean front. As she turned and reentered her cabin there was a knock on her door.

Her breath immediately caught in her throat. It couldn't be.... There was no way he'd do it again, was there? She tightened the tie of her robe and sprinted to the door, throwing it open with a little too much gusto.

Standing outside her room was one of the ship's crewmembers; the young man with the curly hair that had registered her upon arrival. She didn't even try to hide the disappointment that came over her.

"Excuse me, Signorina. I have a message that came for you." Obviously, he hadn't noticed her disappointment because a sweet smile crossed his delicate angel-like face as he held out an envelope for her. Andrea took the envelope and looked at it. As she raised her eyes again toward the young man, he had already strolled halfway down the hall.

"Well, then." She spoke aloud at his wordless retreat, closing the door. "I wonder who sent this."

Andrea sat on the edge of the bed, toying with the corner of the flap. After hesitating for a few minutes, she decided the best thing to do was just open it.

She read: I will meet you in Ville Franche. We can spend the day on the beach. Steve.

Andrea set the down the letter. "Steve?" she whispered in disbelief.

In all truth, she didn't know how she felt about Steve any longer, not to mention his sudden arrival. She should be excited that he finally decided to keep his promise and show up, except she wasn't. No matter how much she tried to muster that excitement, all she felt was indifference.

She secretly wished the message would have been from Lorenzo, but then reality hit. He had his life and job at the vineyard. He was busy, and wasn't about to play babysitter to some jilted tourist. She should be grateful for the time they spent together yesterday and give up thinking about him.

She could have fun with Steve, she told herself as she slipped a flowered sundress on over her bathing suit. There were many times she'd enjoyed Steve's company. He was a likable guy and they had their moments together, but something was different now.

Steve not showing up on the cruise was, as Victoria had said, the last straw. Nevertheless, he was here, now, right? Why didn't he just come aboard? Why did he send a message? Just as quickly as she had thought the questions, she remembered that Lorenzo had the ticket and paperwork that would allow Steve to board the ship. Shit. How would she straighten out this mess? How would she explain to Steve that another person had his ticket? Andrea rubbed her temples. This would prove interesting to say the least. She picked up a tote and tossed in few items she would need for the day: wallet, sunscreen, her ship paperwork. She spied the Botticelli keychain on the bedside table, and just for good measure, threw that in as well. She slipped on her white Keds tennis shoes and glanced one final time around the room making sure she had all she needed. As she exited her cabin and headed toward the disembarking area she paused for a moment and took a deep breath attempting to quell the knot growing in the pit of her stomach before she continued on her way.

* * *

Lorenzo shifted anxiously from leg to leg as he scanned the faces of the people leaving the ship. Contrary to prior sensibilities, he'd driven to France, slept for a few hours in his car, got harassed by a local Constable for doing so, all so he could meet up with Andrea and spend another day with her. What had he been thinking, chasing cruise ships? This was so unlike him. What if Andrea wasn't interested in spending this day with him? What then? He hadn't thought that far in advance. She made him feel so alive yesterday; he wanted to capture that feeling again. Damn but he hope she didn't think him some crazed stalker. She was so unpretentious he found it such a pleasure to be with her. For so long all that occupied his thoughts were the backstabbing, deceitful ways of his ex. He'd become so angry and cold in defense to the pain she caused him, he'd nearly forgotten there were still genuine people left in the world. Odd, but it took one day with a stranger for him to see how closed off and bitter he'd become.

For too many nights he'd laid awake reliving the humiliation and embarrassment of having to tell 300 people, half his friends and family, sitting in the church waiting for his wedding to begin, that the woman supposed to be walking down the aisle as his bride had changed her mind and wasn't coming.

The sea of stunned faces, so full of pity and puzzlement was a vision etched so deep in his psyche it seemed rooted in his very soul. That day was the longest in his life as he stoically accepted the condolences and apologies of the guests, making any and all excuses he could think of, all the while suffering with a million unanswered questions. Her family was equally stunned, and amidst the confusion, made a discrete and hasty exit.

Finding out later she'd been seeing another man and never intended to move to Italy only made the heartache worse. He left the states, returning to his native land, and immersed himself in the family business, and with what wages he'd earned, returning the cost of plane tickets to his family who'd flown all the way from Italy to attend the wedding.

The hard work and long hours kept him too busy and too tired to spend much time dwelling on the past, but the wound was there, festering just under the surface. His grandfather knew. That wise old man knew he still harbored the deep hurt and resentment—which was exactly why he'd sent Lorenzo on the delivery to the ship.

Delivering the dreadful news to the unsuspecting woman forced him to think on his own feelings. His nonno had told him on numerous occasions it was time to let go of the pain and anger, it was time to live again.

It wasn't until this moment as he waited for Andrea that he realized the extent of the burden he carried, simply because of the sudden lightness of his spirit as he stood on this dock, at this port, at this point in his life.

Another group of people leaving the ship caught his attention. As he looked at the passengers excitedly heading off on their day's adventures, he spied one solemn-looking auburn haired woman.

Although she attempted to smile at the people around her, he could see apprehension just behind her gaze. Something bothered her.

"Signorina. Andrea," he called to her, waving his arms to get her attention.

For a brief moment her eyes lit up and a genuine smile crossed her face when she spied him, but it was replaced immediately with a somber expression.

When she reached him, Lorenzo politely kissed each check. "Caio, bella."

"Lorenzo, why are you here?"

"To be honest, I don't know. I surprised myself by coming. I had so much fun yesterday; I thought we could spend today together, also."

She looked up at him then with hazel eyes filled with regret; he felt his heart constrict.

"What is the matter, Andrea? Do you not want to explore France together?"

"Oh, Lorenzo, I would give anything to spend the day with you. It's just... it's just that my... er... the man who...."

"What is it?" He asked, seeing her distress.

"Steve is supposed to meet me here," she finally blurted.

"Steve? The signor who leaves you alone with bottles of wine?"

Andrea began fishing in her bag. "I received a note this morning." She pulled out the crumpled piece of paper that had arrived for her. "He said he would meet me here."

Lorenzo looked at the paper and burst out laughing. He couldn't help himself.

"Ah, bella. Mi dispiace. I'm sorry." He took a breath to settle himself. "I sent that message. I told the ship's crew member I was Steve when I sent you the note in case they checked the paperwork." Lorenzo pulled out the cruise packet from his pocket, waving it before her. "Remember? I'm Steve?"

The moment Andrea heard his explanation and it registered what he had said, he saw the instant release of breath and the sag of her shoulders as realization crossed her face. He noted, as her smile grew, she nearly fell against him with relief.

"You mean Steve isn't really coming?"

"No, bella. Not that I know."

Lorenzo returned her smile.

"I'm sorry to cause you such distress. I thought you would have remembered my having Steve's paperwork."

"It's okay. It's more than okay, believe me."

"Then you will spend the day at the beach with me?" Lorenzo asked.

"Oh yes. I would love that."

Lorenzo noticed how she beamed with newfound happiness. He loved that he was the reason for her mood change.

"Well, then. I do believe the call of the Sirens beckon us to the sea."

* * *

Andrea couldn't have imagined the relief she felt when to her astonishment she ran into Lorenzo instead of Steve and he confessed he wrote the note. She didn't quite know what to make of Lorenzo's spontaneous behavior in driving up to meet the cruise ship in France. The prospect of spending the day with Lorenzo instead of Steve made her happy though. She hadn't quite sorted out her feelings for Steve since he left her alone on the cruise. She recognized the sense of dread she felt thinking it was Steve meeting her, as a clear sign she needed to re-think many things. Nevertheless, for now, she was content to stroll, hand-in-hand with Lorenzo, heading in the direction of the shops that lined the beachfront.

In his hasty decision to drive to France, Lorenzo had not brought any clothes with him or bathing shorts and asked if she minded a shopping excursion before they headed to the water. He wanted to purchase swim trunks and another set of clothes. The alternative, he joked, was swimming in his birthday suit. Andrea laughingly agreed he needed the clothes but secretly thought he'd look pretty good the other way, too.

"Here." Lorenzo stopped outside the entrance of a small shop. "They will have what I need."

Andrea followed Lorenzo inside, watching him walk down the aisles with men's swimwear.

"Bella?" Lorenzo called holding up several swim trunks. He looked to be asking her opinion.

"Either the blue and black one or the yellow," she stated, thinking how either one would go nicely with his dusky Mediterranean coloring.

While he flipped through the racks a short distance away, Andrea found herself scanning a row of shirts before her. Right in front of her was a lovely, white linen shirt she thought would look perfect on him over the khaki shorts he had picked out to try on. She pulled out the garment, running her fingers along the fine material, an image of him standing on the beach, with the ocean breeze molding the shirt against his—

"Should I get that one also?"

"Huh? Oh." Andrea collected her thoughts. She had been so lost in her daydream she hadn't heard Lorenzo come up behind her. "I think it's a lovely shirt, but you don't...." Lorenzo cut off her remaining words taking the garment from her hand, checking the size and putting it in his arm with the other clothes he would take to the dressing room. Andrea took a breath. *Whew.* Almost got caught thinking those sexy thoughts.

"I think this is enough for now. Let me try these on." Lorenzo headed toward the dressing rooms. "I'll only be a moment longer, bella," he called.

"No worry, take your time." Andrea wandered up and down several aisles of clothing as she waited for him.

True to his word, he was only a few more moments, coming out of the dressing room with a navy tee over the swim trunks.

"I will wear these, now," he told the clerk, handing her the tags that came off the clothing.

"Now you look like you're ready for the beach." Andrea smiled waiting as he paid for his clothing.

"We have only one more stop I'd like to make, in a shop we passed on the way. Then we'll head back to the automobile and—"

"I thought we were going to the beach."

"We are."

Lorenzo grabbed Andrea's hand and lead her out of the shop, heading back in the direction they had come.

Several shops down, Lorenzo turned and then led her inside a café. The moment they entered the shop, he spoke French to the clerk. Andrea understood the clerk agreed with Lorenzo by the nod of his head and the occasional "oui" but again had no idea what Lorenzo had asked the man. After a brief conversation, the clerk turned and began doing whatever it was Lorenzo had requested.

"You speak French, too?" Andrea asked, amazed.

"Just a little. It's not too different than Italian." Lorenzo took her elbow. "Come, sit. It will take them a few moments to get our lunch ready."

"You ordered lunch?"

"Si. I thought we'd have a picnic on the beach."

"Lorenzo, how thoughtful. That would be great." Lorenzo's thoughtfulness once again delighted Andrea. This was so out of the scope of Steve's behavior. In all fairness, Steve wasn't mean and he didn't forget special occasions, but often Andrea got the feeling he only remembered them because his assistant reminded him. He never did anything spontaneous and without prior planning. God, but Lorenzo was a nice change.

Once their lunch had been prepared and packaged up for them to take, Lorenzo took her hand and lead Andrea away from the tourist shopping area toward his car.

"I know of a wonderful beach, less crowded, just a ways from here," he explained as they reached his car and he held open the door for her.

"Great," Andrea agreed, slipping into the passenger seat. She couldn't seem to take her eyes off Lorenzo as he strolled around the front of the car and slid into the driver side, start the motor, and pull out onto the road. He had such a calm, relaxed manner; Andrea found it pleasant to simply watch him. She found herself smiling at that thought. Lorenzo glanced over to her and smiled back. *If he only knew*, she thought.

They weren't in the car long before Lorenzo pulled into a parking area more rustic and less touristy than where they had come. There were only a half dozen or so other cars parked alongside them.

"The water is just over that hill," Lorenzo explained, coming around to open Andrea's door for her.

After waiting a moment for Lorenzo to put his new clothes in the trunk and take out a small blanket and their lunch, Andrea followed

Lorenzo toward the beach. Once they crested the hill, Andrea was surprised to see a beautiful expanse of beach right before her. Lorenzo had been right, this stretch of beach was nearly deserted.

"How did you know about this place?" Andrea asked as they strolled closer to the shore.

"I didn't until today. I found it on my way here. I needed a place to rest and happened to stumble on it. I met another couple early this morning who told me that it was a public beach.

"Wow. It's beautiful. Perfect."

"Si. The ocean is rather breathtaking, no?"

Lorenzo spread out the blanket and set down their lunch bag. Andrea watched him look out over the water, the breeze whipping his hair away from his angular face. He took a deep breath, inhaling the salty scent, before he tugged up his T-shirt, pulling it over his head intent on going swimming.

Andrea's gaze fixed on his tan, muscular arms and chest, made hard, she suspected, by his work at the vineyard. God, his body was firm and perfectly built, not that Steve wasn't athletic, but Lorenzo was in great shape. She swallowed, letting her eyes travel over the entire expanse of his torso before moving her gaze out to the water. She shouldn't be thinking these things about him. He was a great companion. Nothing more. They lived in two opposite parts of the world, and technically, she was still in a relationship with Steve. She mustn't allow her attraction to Lorenzo get in the way of that. Still, he was a fine sight, she thought rubbing down the goose flesh on her arms.

"Are you coming, bella? I'm sure the water will be refreshing."

"Oh. Yes. I was just admiring the view." Okay, so that sounded rather like an innuendo. "I mean, the ocean is so different than the lake back home." Andrea watched as he winked, then turned and started walking toward the water.

She untied the shoulder straps of her dress and let it fall to the sand around her feet. She stepped over it, kicking off her tennis shoes and followed Lorenzo. He dove under the water and surfaced a moment later flinging his hair back.

"Ooooooh!" She squealed as the initial chill of a wave hit her.

"You get used to it," he said, coming back to get her.

Andrea watched his gaze slide over her from head to toe before his eyes met hers.

"Bella." He smiled affectionately and

reached for her hand. "You are a beautiful woman."

Warmth flooded her cheeks at his compliment. *Oh God.* Never had a simple compliment sent such shivers through her. Her immediate and intense attraction to Lorenzo was disconcerting but not unappreciated. She often wished she could muster some of those hormone-inspired feelings when it came to Steve. However, then Steve never complemented her with such charm and obvious desire. Lorenzo was certainly tempting with his sexy Italian magnetism. She could sure get lost in those dark dreamy eyes.

And what's wrong with that? A little voice in the back of her mind whispered. Before she could answer that voice, Lorenzo tugged her farther out into the water until it became deep enough she could swim. Andrea dove under and a second later came up sputtering as Lorenzo reached out to steady her.

"I forgot about it being salt water. Blah." Andrea spat, noticing the grin on Lorenzo's face as she did.

"You're laughing at me?"

Lorenzo's hearty chuckle greeted her ears.

"You are." Andrea splashed water at Lorenzo.

Lorenzo sent a spray of water right back in

her direction, squarely soaking her. He continued to laugh.

"Hey. Not fair." Andrea returned his splash with one of her own but not nearly as accurate as his and throwing her off balance in the process. She fell back into the water, squealing.

Lorenzo reached for her, pulling her up and at the same time a wave jostled her off her feet and Andrea fell against him. Lorenzo's quick action caught her, but instead of setting her back on her feet, his arm slid around her and held her tightly against his hard, wet body.

Andrea's breath caught in her throat at the sudden contact. She froze. A thousand thoughts filled her brain on how to handle the situation. Despite knowing what she should do, Andrea did not move. The undeniable truth was she liked the way she felt in Lorenzo's arms. This wasn't like her. She just didn't go around hugging men she'd just met, yet that is exactly what she was doing, and on top of that, she hadn't attempted to remove herself from his embrace.

Her hesitancy sent the wrong message, and there was a very distinct possibility Lorenzo would misinterpret her reluctance to move away from him as wanting more from him. God help her. She wanted more from him.

That confession stunned her. In the past, she'd never consider jeopardizing a relationship for a moment of passion with a stranger. Then she reminded herself, other than an occasional goodwill gesture, what kind of relationship did she really have with Steve? He was virtually nonexistent, and the feelings coursing through her at this moment were very, *very* real.

Any further thoughts abruptly halted as Lorenzo lowered his lips over hers.

"If you want me to stop, say it now, cara, or I am going to kiss you." He whispered against her mouth.

Andrea remained silent, her pulse racing. Her chest rose with more frequent intervals to accommodate her quickening breath. Anticipation flooded through her. Still, she said nothing, but chose that moment to raise her gaze to Lorenzo's, to meet dark eyes smoldering with desire.

"Time's up," he informed her. His mouth skimmed over hers a split second before his lips captured hers in a deep, scorching kiss.

All thoughts stopped. Her brain ceased to function. Only two things registered at that moment, the fervent pounding of her heart and the overwhelming passion rising within her.

He kissed her long and deep, encouraging

her to accept his exploration of her mouth with his tongue. She didn't cower away, but instead met his kiss with equal passion, melting further into his arms, clutching his shoulders.

If she didn't know any better, she would say her reaction to Lorenzo was divinely inspired, but more likely her heightened state was due to the seduction of a foreign country, not having sex—in like forever—Lorenzo's super sex appeal or the fact that was one hell of a good kiss.

Andrea was breathless when she pulled back and looked up at Lorenzo.

"Wow," she whispered.

Andrea wasn't too embarrassed for muttering her feelings when she noted an equally stunned expression graced Lorenzo's face. He clearly was not unaffected by their kiss and stroked her face gently as composure once again settled over him.

There wasn't time to dwell on the kiss as Lorenzo righted her and led her back toward shore, keeping his hand on the small of her back to steady her against the waves until they were out of the water.

They sat on the blanket together while Lorenzo took out the lunch. He poured a glass of wine for her in the plastic cups provided by the cafe and set out grapes, cheese, and slices of a particular sausage she found delicious.

In between bites of food, they took turns taking photos on their phones and swapping phone numbers and then when they were full and feeling relaxed they both lay back on the blanket to nap in the hot Riviera sun.

Nap? Was she kidding? Her body was on fire for this sexy man, the sun only added to her overall warmth and arousal. Despite drinking a half bottle of wine, Andrea had never felt more awake than she did right now. Just the presence of his nearly naked body lying alongside her kept her skin alert and tingling. These sensations were new to her. She'd never felt this way with Steve, and her unexpected attraction to this man held her enthralled.

After a long stretch of quiet, lazy moments, Lorenzo leaned up on his elbow, garnering her attention by his movement. He gazed down at her.

"This morning as you were coming off the ship, you were visibly upset thinking you were meeting Steve."

Andrea didn't deny his statement. She had been upset.

"Yes."

"Do you still want to be with him?"

Lorenzo surprised her with his direct question. "I don't know. I mean, Steve isn't a bad guy; he's just preoccupied with his job. He does put his work ahead of me. I have been reevaluating our relationship, yes. I was upset because I didn't want a confrontation to mar my vacation. He did, after all, leave me alone."

Lorenzo was silent for a long moment. He absently touched her shoulder, his fingers drawing tiny circles on her skin. He seemed momentarily withdrawn into his thoughts.

"When I told you I came back to Italy because I was needed at the vineyard... that wasn't the whole truth."

"What happened to bring you home?"

"My fiancée left me at the altar on our wedding day. I came back to Italy to put the whole ordeal behind me."

Andrea sat up and faced him. "Oh Lorenzo, that must have been devastating."

"Si. It wasn't pleasant. But I'm telling you this because when I brought you the flowers and wine, I understood your disappointment."

"So we are kindred spirits, the two of us?"

"Si."

"I am so sorry that happened to you, Lorenzo."

"Grazie, bella. And I am sorry you were left on the cruise."

Andrea smiled, noticing Lorenzo's confused expression when she did.

"But we wouldn't have met each other," she said, explaining her reason for smiling.

"True, bella. True. And I have enjoyed these past two days."

"Me too, Lorenzo.

Lorenzo leaned in, and without giving her the choice whether to say no or not, he kissed her.

Andrea found this kiss as unexpected and erotic as his earlier one, and once again, her inability to resist surprised her. This time, however, she didn't hesitate to kiss him back. In all actuality, Andrea couldn't wrap her head around how easily she succumbed to Lorenzo. It didn't matter they had just met. Andrea was living in the moment, and this very moment Lorenzo made her feel sexy and alive and she was on fire for this man. When he slipped his tongue inside her mouth, she capitulated to whatever would happen.

He nipped and kissed her lips, neck and ears, until she found herself melting against him. He eased her back on the blanket, situating himself gently but eagerly over her. He trailed his fingers along her face and neck sliding lower to her chest. She must have stiffened a little, because he moved his face next to hers and whispered, "No one can see, cara."

Lorenzo's fingers slid over the swell of her breasts to the edge of her bikini top and then slipped inside. He caressed one nipple slowly, tantalizingly and Andrea couldn't help the sigh that escaped her throat.

As he continued to caress her breast, his lips continued their foray along her face and neck drawing her further and further into her desire. Somewhere in her stupor, she realized Lorenzo had moved aside her bathing suit top and bared her breasts. He lowered his face to her chest, capturing one peaked nipple between his teeth. Once again, the sensations this man wrought inside her swelled in epic proportions and she didn't care if the entire country of France watched, because right now only one thing mattered.

Although Andrea felt quite selfish in her need, she noted Lorenzo didn't seem to mind. He was quite intent to explore every inch of her with his mouth and fingers, and as much as she returned his caresses, he made it very clear this was about her and lifted her hands over her head where he held onto them, preventing her from touching him.

Damn, but as unfair as this was, she hungrily took what he gave because she felt quite decadent in her sexuality and reality was, after today she would probably never see

Lorenzo again.

"Oh cara, you are beautiful," Lorenzo whispered in between kisses, further adding to the head-spinning passion soaring through her. He was sure good for her spirit as well as her libido. His words sent spirals of warmth flowing through her, gathering at the juncture of her thighs. Geez, but she was soaking, so near release from just his kisses.

"Open your eyes," Lorenzo instructed. "I want to watch you as you come."

"But I'm not—" Her words ceased mid-sentence at the touch of his hand slipping inside her bathing suit bottoms. His fingers gently slid inside the folds of her sex, stroking her until she was near writhing in his arms. While his hand brought her closer and closer to her orgasm, his mouth continued lavishing her breasts.

Shit, this man was good and she was damn sure going to see this elicit tryst to its completion. In a matter of minutes, she was panting and quaking in his arms, rocked by an earth-shattering orgasm all the while looking into his desire-laden gaze.

Andrea could feel Lorenzo hard and throbbing against her hip, so she reached for him. As her fingers brushed against the swollen material of his bathing suit, he shook his head.

"No, cara. Not now." He kissed her.

Her face must have shown her confusion because he smiled, easing her concern.

Andrea didn't pretend to understand what his denial was all about, but his smile told her all was well, so she smiled back and accepted his behavior.

Lorenzo gave her shoulder a gentle squeeze and lay back on the blanket. Andrea now sat up, her gaze drifting from Lorenzo to the ocean

Did she really just let this man give her an orgasm? Holy shit but did he have a charisma that drew her to him like a magnet. Her body still shivered from the intimacy she'd shared with this man. The old adage of Italian men being romantic was certainly true as far as she was concerned. She was undeniably attracted to him. He was handsome and sexual and nice, all rolled into one package. In addition, as much as she told herself not to, she was falling for him.

A pang of sadness swept through her. She would miss him. She would be forever grateful to this once complete stranger for helping her get over the heartache of Steve leaving her alone, because Lorenzo understood what it was like.

Lorenzo pushed up onto his elbows. "Let's

go for a quick swim then get dinner before you have to return," he suggested, rubbing her arm.

"I like that idea." Andrea agreed, grateful to set aside her thoughts for the time being.

Lorenzo rose and offered his hand to help her. He didn't release her hand, though, and held it until they reached the water's edge and the jostling of the waves made it impossible for him continue holding it.

They splashed and swam for a short while before returning to the car and heading out to find a restaurant.

Dinner was pleasant enough, but a feeling of melancholy took root and grew inside Andrea as the evening progressed. She couldn't help be sad that tonight might be the last time they'd see each other. To hope there could be anything more to their unexpected friendship would be ridiculous. She thought she could make herself believe this, but as the evening drew to a close, Andrea found she could not ignore the sadness gnawing at her.

"I hope you keep in touch, Lorenzo," Andrea said as they walked hand in hand back toward the ship's dock. "These last two days have been so special. You've made my vacation a memorable one. Thank you from the bottom of my heart."

"Si, bella. I too have enjoyed our time

together."

Andrea felt her throat constrict. She refused to cry. *Keep it light,* she told herself. *Don't make a fool of yourself in front of him.*

They stopped at the bottom of the ship's gangway. Lorenzo took both of her hands and turned to look at her. "I will not forget these two days, bella. You have lightened my spirit by allowing me to share my culture and country with you. For this I will be forever grateful." He bent and kissed each of her cheeks, then straightened, taking a step back. Andrea looked up at him, unable to speak, hoping her smile conveyed her appreciation for what he had done for her.

"Take care, Lorenzo. I will think about you each time I purchase a bottle of your wine," she teased.

Lorenzo smiled, but Andrea noticed the smile didn't pull at the corners of his eyes as it had done the first time she'd noticed it. He let her hands drop. "Arrivederci, Andrea." He nodded, stepping back another step.

"Good-bye," she whispered, turning away.

Andrea had only taken several timid strides up the ramp when she heard Lorenzo call her name. She turned just as he ran up to her and pulled her against his body, gathering her into his strong arms. His actions caught her totally off guard and she never had a second to think about what happened as he swiftly covered her mouth with his in a deep, searing kiss.

Andrea found herself clutching his shirt as he deepened the kiss, exploring her mouth with his tongue, eliciting a moan from her she didn't expect. Oh God, but did his kiss do things to her. Somewhere the fabled fireworks were going off, or maybe her heart pounded. It was hard to tell. His hands slid over her as if he were committing to memory every inch of her. Oh, he tasted good, and when she took a moment to breathe and stare into those dark eyes of his, they were so telling of his desire. "Lorenzo...." she sighed, a moment before he moved away.

His departure was abrupt and unexpected, and for a moment Andrea wasn't sure what happened had actually happened. As he walked away, she felt the emptiness multiplying inside her. Rubbing her arms against the unexpected chill that crept over her skin, she pondered why he would kiss her like that and then leave. She had to admit, it was some memorable way to say farewell, one she'd not likely forget.

Andrea took a minute to compose herself before she thought to move. Lorenzo's kiss had left her so weak kneed, she wanted to make sure the blood circulated again before attempting to take a step. She found herself sucking in several deep breaths to calm her racing heart. No kiss had ever affected her this way, especially one from someone she had only known for two days, and someone she'd never see again. Her heart sank at that thought as she looked up at the ship and began what seemed like an endless journey up the gangway.

Chapter Five

Lorenzo made the final snip on a tangle of grape vines he'd spent all morning pruning. Gathering the trimmings, he threw them into the back of the ATV he used to travel the fields. He set the shears down on the hood and slipped into the seat, wiping his brow. He reached for and twisted the top off a bottle of water from the cooler he carried, and swallowed half of it down before stopping to breathe.

Dropping his gaze to the phone propped on the dash, he touched the screen. The photograph of he and Andrea taken in the Medici Chapels stared back at him. He took another drink of water, never taking his eyes off the picture.

Her smile, her eyes, her full breasts, the way she sighed when she came.... Lord help him but he hadn't stopped thinking of Andrea since he left her at the dock the previous night. He drove all through the night with the taste of her still fresh on his lips, tempting him to throw propriety out the window and run back to her. He didn't know what compelled him to take her in his arms for that final kiss, but whatever it was, it had nearly consumed him. She'd felt so good in his arms, he almost hadn't let her go. When she looked up at him with those passion-laden eyes; well, that had been his undoing.

He wanted her so badly on the beach yesterday as he pleasured her. However, that would have been too obvious to the other swimmers and bathers. As it was, the control he mustered to bring her to orgasm took such will power, if she had touched him, he would have come in her hand right then and there; the other bathers would have had quite a show. If he had made love with her, he would not have been able to leave her. She was the kind of woman a man held onto once he found her, and he knew that was impossible.

There was more about Andrea than physical attraction that enthralled him. She was so genuine and sincere he couldn't help be drawn to her. She helped him in ways she would never know. She was a balm that healed his soul and allowed him to put his past behind him. She helped him to find life and joy again, and he hadn't intended on ever finding someone who could do that. He so badly wanted to run to her, grab her up into his arms again, swing her around and confess how she made him feel.

Lorenzo sighed.

That moment had passed. He'd been afraid to reveal how he felt. Afraid she would think him a love-starved fool. Afraid she'd think two days wasn't enough to feel connected to someone. Just afraid of being rejected. Again. Now, as swiftly as she entered his life, she was gone and here he was alone again.

Lorenzo picked up his phone. He was so tempted to text her, to confess he missed her. If her kiss indicated her feelings, then he was positive of her feelings for him. She was instantly soft and receptive the moment his lips touched hers.

He set down his phone. *What the hell. I'm acting like an idiot.* Lorenzo took one final swig from his water bottle, dismissing his befuddled state. He started the ATV and continued with his inspection of the crops, pushing aside any inclination to contact her.

Lorenzo made it as far as two more rows of grapes before he slammed on the brakes, sending a cloud of dust pluming behind the vehicle. He picked up the phone, stared at it. In one decisive moment he opened up the text message screen, searched for Andrea's number and typed: *I miss you. Tell me you miss me. Is there a chance for us?* His thumb hovered over the "send" button for a moment before brevity won out and he tapped the screen, sending the message.

* * *

Andrea turned the key in the lock and stepped inside the ship's cabin. Closing and locking the door and kicking off her shoes, she fell back on the bed, letting out a weary breath.

What a long day. Her feet were aching from an all-day walking tour of Valencia. Exhaustion overwhelmed her. She thought if she could keep herself busy, if she could keep her mind occupied, then she wouldn't think about Lorenzo. And while that seemed great in theory, the reality was, he continued to fill her thoughts, even as she visited the beautiful Serranos Towers, the Grail Church, and a host of other wonderful ancient buildings.

Her whole body still tingled from yesterday afternoon's encounter and then the incredible kiss he surprised her with on the gangway last evening. His sudden show of affection so completely stunned her, she hadn't even tried to call after him. She just let him leave.

Andrea sighed. Probably just as well, considering she already had someone in her life—or was *supposed* to have someone in her life. Lorenzo would only complicate an already screwed up relationship with Steve. And thinking of Steve. Not one word from him. Not an "I miss you," or "Are you having a good time?" He even went so far as to put international calling on her phone the last time he traveled overseas so they could stay in touch. However, there were no messages from him this time except the flowers and the wine. Perhaps he expected her to text first, allowing her time to forgive him for not showing. Andrea closed her eyes. Would she forgive Steve or was this time the last? Was it selfish to want someone who liked being with her?

She wished she had stopped Lorenzo from leaving. The melancholy she tried so hard to ignore all day gnawed at her more than ever. Despite the fact she was committed to Steve, it was Lorenzo she thought of now.

Andrea pushed herself off the bed. Maybe a relaxing shower would help clear her thoughts.

* * *

Coming out of the bathroom, towel drying her hair, Andrea had second thoughts about contacting Steve. After all, he'd paid for the trip. The least she could do would be to thank him and find out if he would be joining her. She emptied her bag on the bed, fishing through the contents for her phone. She spied her camera and picked it up, making sure she had turned it off. She was glad she remembered it today. She took some beautiful photos of the buildings she visited. Good thing she brought it, as her phone memory card was almost full. When she got home, she would be sure to transfer photos to her computer.

Andrea found her phone and turned it on. She had one text message she'd get to after she called Steve. She dialed his familiar number and waited. *Voicemail.* No surprise. She hung up, disappointed. *Typical*, she thought, sighing.

Andrea moved the phone back so she could see who'd texted her. When she read the contact name, her heart skipped a beat. *Lorenzo.* She pushed the buttons that would take her to his message and sat stunned after reading the three simple lines: *I miss you. Tell me you miss me. Is there a chance for us?* The pounding of her heart was deafening.

Oh my.

Chapter Six

Lorenzo tugged up the duffel bag strap on his shoulder, shifting his weight to his other leg as he waited impatiently to board the plane to Ibiza, Spain. This was the last flight available that would allow him to arrive in time to catch the cruise ship and Andrea at that port. Despite his anxiety, the spontaneity of this trip filled him with excitement. Andrea didn't expect him.

After making every excuse he could think of yesterday for why she hadn't answered his text, he had almost accepted the cold hard truth that she might not be interested in him the way he was interested in her. Rejection was tough to swallow a second time. He had checked his phone a hundred times during the day while he worked the fields, hoping for one text from Andrea, but each minute she hadn't returned his message was met with disappointment. As the day wore on, he grew more disillusioned that maybe he had been imaging what he thought he felt between them. By the time day turned to night he'd given up hope of hearing from her and after a quick dinner with his grandparents, he held the sinking feeling he wouldn't. Damn but something was between them, he just hoped she would recognize it and take a chance with him.

When the phone finally made the telltale chime that he'd received a message much later that night, he practically flew to retrieve it from where it rested on the coffee table. After waiting all day, he found himself pausing, bracing for the worst before opening the text from Andrea....

I do miss you, too. I don't know how it could be possible after knowing you such a short time. What shall we do? I just turned on my phone. Forgive me.

Forgiven. You drove me crazy all day thinking you didn't want to talk to me.

Just the opposite.

I'm glad, cara.

We do need to talk, Lorenzo.

I agree, but for now, you get some sleep. We'll talk tomorrow.

Good night, Lorenzo.

Good night, cara.

Lorenzo smiled to himself recalling the text conversation and enjoying the prospect of surprising her, today. He would definitely show her a great time, taking her to dinner and then to some of the famous dance clubs on the island, and then, well, he'd like to spend some private time with her, showing her a great time in other ways.

He was better prepared to spend a few days with her, this time sporting several change of clothes as well a couple bottles of his wine as a gift.

Once finally settled on the plane, Lorenzo shot off a quick text to Andrea asking her what her plans were for the day. She replied right away, stating she planned to shop in D'Alt Villa.

After telling her to have fun, he settled in for the flight.

* * *

Andrea strolled in and out of the quaint shops near the port, purchasing a few items she would give as gifts to Victoria and Steve. She shrugged off the idea of going to one of the beautiful beaches, as it wasn't much fun going alone as with someone, and *the* someone she wanted to be with was in Italy, and the someone she was supposed to be with was in the United States. *Wow*, she thought, realizing how lonely she felt.

Andrea sighed. She did long to see Lorenzo again, especially after they both admitted missing each other. Now what? They were still countries apart, but damn, did she miss being with him. She had more fun with him in two days than she had with Steve over the past year. That alone was in his favor. However, the fact he lived so far away would be a difficult obstacle. She wasn't interested in having a part-time boyfriend. She already had that. Still, every time she thought about Lorenzo and the way he had touched her and the kiss he left her with, she couldn't help but want to be with him. She didn't see how that could work, however.

Maybe she should have never answered his text. Admitting her feelings only complicated matters. She chalked up her candidness to the whimsical fantasies of being on vacation in a foreign country where real life seemed so far away and flirting with an attractive Italian guy she'd likely never see again seemed safe.

She really needed to push all of that out of her mind now, and just enjoy what was left of her vacation. As if to validate her new inner strength, she pulled out her phone and dialed Steve's number. Again, she received his voice mail, but this time she left him a message: "Hi, it's me. Just thinking of you and thought I'd call and say hello. Hope you're not working too hard. See you soon."

Before she put her phone away, however, Andrea flipped to her photo gallery and paused on a picture another tourist had taken of her and Lorenzo standing by the statue of David. She ran her fingers over the screen, touching his hair and face longingly before closing the phone and sliding it back into her bag.

A few minutes later, as Andrea stood in a small shop contemplating a purchase for Steve, her phone rang. She stepped outside to answer it, seeing it was from Lorenzo.

"Cara."

"Lorenzo, we need to rethink—" His next statement cut off her remaining words.

"I have a surprise for you. Back at the ship."

"Lorenzo...."

"Seriously, cara. When will you return?"

"In a bit. Why? What is it?"

"Me."

"What?" Andrea was stunned.

"Si. I came to Spain."

"Y-you're here? Really?"

"Si. I am on the ship. I wanted to see you again."

"I'm on my way."

Andrea's good intentions of trying to push Lorenzo from her mind flew right out the door the moment she learned he was here to see her. She forgot all about the purchase for Steve in her haste to head back to the ship and meet with Lorenzo. She was so surprised to find him here, wanting to see her, her heart soared with possibilities again. Forget what she'd been thinking only moments ago. None of those thoughts mattered now.

Andrea sprinted up the gangway, stopping only long enough to show her identification allowing her to board the ship. She scanned the passenger area and spied him immediately.

"Lorenzo," she called to him, waving. The smile he flashed her when he turned and saw her coming toward him was enough to melt her heart.

"Cara," he said, pulling her into his arms as she reached him. "I thought never to hold you again," he whispered against her ear just before his lips found hers, kissing her tenderly. Andrea returned his kiss with equal affection, surprised by how easily she went to him.

Andrea melted into Lorenzo's embrace

and had to use all her will power to end the kiss and step back. She met his gaze.

"I could not stay away. You have captured me, cara."

"And you me. But this puts us in quite a predicament, Lorenzo."

"Si, cara," he agreed. "But tonight and the next three days, let's put aside all doubts. There will be time soon when we must talk of these things, but for now, I just want to take you dancing in the famous discothèques. I want nothing more than to spend time with you."

Andrea looked at the man standing before her and noted she wanted the same. The prospect of enjoying life to the fullest with Lorenzo for the next three days sounded extremely appealing. A prospect she realized she would not pass up no matter the consequences. She was here to have a good time, and her good time stood right next to her, equally prepared to enjoy their time together.

"Agreed. Let's go dancing." She spoke with no hesitation.

* * *

The nightlife in Ibiza was a flurry of activity. Dance clubs graced every corner, and people, both locals and tourists, crowded the streets with celebratory air. Music filled the streets as Lorenzo and Andrea made their way to yet another club. This would make the third one they'd visited. Lorenzo was determined Andrea experience several of the more popular clubs. The last one they headed toward had a reputation for its Latin/world flair. It was by far the trendiest of them all and definitely captured the euphoric atmosphere of the island.

Lorenzo smiled down at Andrea as they walked. She was beautiful, all flushed from the sun and the dancing. She wore a short black dress that clung to her like a second skin, accentuating her curves and feminine features. He was half-crazy with want for this woman. She was sexy and smart and fun all rolled into one. He slipped his arm around her, pulling her close as they entered the club. He loved the way she felt against him. She fit him perfectly in so many ways.

They made their way toward the crowded dance floor, slipping into the throng of people twisting and gyrating to the hypnotic beat of the music. They too found themselves caught up in the sensual trance-like rhythms that surrounded them. Lorenzo could see why people were attracted to this club. The sultry music and charged atmosphere was pulsing, seeping with eroticism. Lorenzo moved closer to Andrea so the lengths of their bodies slid over each other as they danced. The feel of her against him was enticing. He was hard and aroused in a matter of minutes.

The stain on her cheeks and the taught peaks of her luscious bosom indicated Andrea felt the same. Lorenzo turned her around in his arms, so his hips ground against her backside, and his hands slid over her waist to her breasts. He cupped her breasts as their hips swayed in unison to the beat of the music. He lowered his mouth to her neck, where he placed kisses.

"You feel so good all aroused and soft in my arms, cara. Just like at the beach the other day."

Andrea tilted her head back, looked up at him, and smiled. He could see the desire in her eyes, and loved that he was the source of her passion. "I will make such sweet love to you tonight you will never want to leave my arms." He spoke openly of his intent. After all, placing his travel bag in her room earlier implied he would stay with her. Worried for a moment his boldness may have taken Andrea aback, he turned her enough to see her face. She raised her eyebrows in a question, and then smiled.

"That is quite a boast, Lorenzo." Andrea chuckled, still moving against him.

"That is not a boast, but a promise."

"Ah, you Italian men, you have such reputations as lovers."

Lorenzo smiled, proudly. "There are worse things in life than to enjoy romance, cara."

"It is this place, the city, the music. It's magic."

"The magic is you, cara."

Andrea looked as if she wanted to say something else, but an inebriated patron interrupted any further conversation by almost spilling his drink on Andrea when he bumped her in passing. Lorenzo's quick thinking and action of swinging her around, kept the accident at a minimum.

"Lorenzo, let's leave. I'd like to walk on the shore and cool off."

"Si. I too would like a quieter place."

Lorenzo took her hand, and together, they wove their way through the crowd and out of the club.

"Whew. I didn't realize how warm it was in there. The breeze feels good."

"The beach is just ahead. We can sit and listen to the waves."

Lorenzo and Andrea strolled along the sand of the empty beach, shoes in hand, laughing as they dodged the splashing waves. They found themselves on a secluded stretch of sand away from the hustle and bustle of the city proper. Lorenzo took Andrea's hand and led her to a small copse of palm trees, away from the shore and the water. They sat together, Andrea leaning against Lorenzo. He wrapped his arms around her.

"I can't believe you're here," Andrea said, in reference to his spontaneous trip to see her.

"Si. I couldn't be without you."

"I want you to know; it means a lot that you came all this way to be with me."

"I am glad to be here." Lorenzo reached out and cupped her face, turning her head. He placed his lips on hers; kissing her long and deep until they were both near breathless.

"I want you, cara, right now, without regard to where we are or who might pass."

"I want you too."

Lorenzo lowered his lips to hers again as she turned in his arms.

* * *

Andrea shivered but not from the cold. She surprised even herself by her candor, but damn, after all the intimate dancing with this sexy man, her body was on fire with need. Never had she been so completely willing for the touch of ecstasy.

Maybe it was the music or the allure of the island, or even the fact Lorenzo came all this way to see her. Whatever it was, her passion completely consumed her.

She rose and knelt next to Lorenzo, cupping his face in her hands. She looked at him. He was stunningly handsome with his tan complexion and dark eyes. He was every fantasy she had imagined on dark, lonely nights when Steve was away. Lorenzo had said the next few days were for them, and Andrea would take full advantage of their short time together. Never had she wanted Steve with as much fervor as she felt now for Lorenzo. Steve's indifference to her finally made her realize she needed excitement and adventure and maybe even something a bit decadent. Her boring life was plain and she was tired of it. Victoria's words came back to her: *You are a vibrant woman wasting the best years of your life waiting around for something that's not going to happen.*

How those words stuck her. She had been waiting, wasting so many years, and she just didn't have it in her to wait any longer. She needed this man to remind her what passion was and all it could be.

Andrea leaned into Lorenzo and kissed him fervently. "Make love to me. Here. Now," she murmured against his lips.

"Ah, cara," he sighed, kissing her neck, as Andrea moved to straddle his lap, hiking her skirt higher. The sensation of Lorenzo's lips caressing the curve of her neck sent tendrils of warmth deep into her belly. His hands, slid over her breasts and midriff, then back to her breasts again. His mouth found hers once more and he thrust his tongue inside with purposeful intent. As he kissed her, his hand slid to her hips, grasping each side of her and pulling her down against his hardness.

Andrea tugged at his shirt, pulling it free from his pants. She slid her hands up under the cotton fabric, skimming her fingers over the firm muscles of his stomach and chest. Gliding her fingertips over his taught nipples, a moan from deep within his throat and a deeper thrust of his tongue rewarded her exploration.

One of Lorenzo's hands threaded in her hair, keeping her face close to his; the other slid to her shoulder, pulling down the strap of her dress to rest at her elbow. The dress loosened enough for him to slide his hand inside her neckline and grasp her breast. Her nipples became hard instantly and she couldn't help pushing into his hand. She never wanted him to stop touching her.

Andrea sat up, looking down at Lorenzo's

sex-laden gaze. His eyes were deep and languid and so filled with desire, the heat coiled even tighter in her center. He lifted his other hand and slipped the second strap of her dress off her shoulder, drawing her dress downward to expose her breasts. She watched as he undressed her, stroking one breast then the other.

It wasn't until he closed his mouth around one of her nipples that she closed her eyes and let her head fall forward. The erotic sensation of his warm tongue circling her erect nipple completely overwhelmed her. Lorenzo moved his mouth to her other breast, giving it as much attention as the first, pausing only long enough to kiss her mouth before returning to her breasts.

She was on fire. The passionate nature of this man completely undid her and provided her with brevity she normally kept hidden. Sex with Steve was nice but uneventful, certainly not the mind blowing, sweaty passion she was experiencing with Lorenzo. She liked this daring, abandoned sex.

Andrea lowered her hand between them, rubbing the erection straining against his jeans. He shifted beneath her, allowing her more access, but it wasn't enough. She wanted him, in the flesh, straining against her hand.

She tugged at the snap on the waistband of his jeans and slid the zipper downward, pushing the material aside to free him. She heard the intake of breath hissed between his teeth as she took hold of him. There was no leisure in the way she wanted this man, her movements urgent and precise. He firm cock throbbed against her palm, and Lorenzo's increased breaths between kisses revealed he too was lost in the passion.

"Bella, I didn't bring—" his sentence cut short by her reply.

"I'm on the pill and clean. You?" Her question was hot against his face.

"Si."

Andrea felt Lorenzo's hands once again on each side of her hips, only this time he slid up her dress, revealing her thong beneath. He pushed aside the small piece of fabric, caressing her before sliding a finger deeper between her folds, stroking her into near mindlessness.

This time is was Andrea who moaned against his face, unable to hide the pleasure she derived from his touch.

"Oh God, Lorenzo," she sighed, wanting nothing less than this man inside her. Now!

When Lorenzo slipped a finger inside her, she nearly came undone, tensing around him, trying desperately not to let go just yet. She rose onto her knees, positioning herself over his erection as she shifted; he removed his hand and eased his hardness inside her. She slid down on his length.

Oh God, he felt so good, she thought as he moved beneath her. Lorenzo wrapped his arms around her, holding her tight, helping her move on him. Andrea found her hands in his hair, holding his head against her breast as she quickened her movements.

"Come for me, cara," Lorenzo whispered.

He couldn't have said anything more sexy or arousing and Andrea felt her body respond to his request. She felt him thrust into her with insistent movements equal to her own, unrelenting in his own need. She was so hotly aroused, so lost in the moment, her body exploded with wild abandon, tensing and quaking for endless moments as Lorenzo swelled, plunged vigorously, and came deep inside her.

She didn't move. Couldn't move. Her body continued to tremble from the intensity of what they just shared. Lorenzo kept himself inside her, moving in a slow unhurried grind, prolonging the dreamy languor of afterglow. He lifted his head from her chest and gazed into her face. Andrea thought he was about to say something, but instead, he pulled her face to his and kissed her oh so tenderly. She felt her heart constrict at the loving gesture. She was falling for this man, and no matter what she told herself about the logistics of such a relationship, her heart would have none of it.

"Lorenzo."

He put his fingers to her lips. "Shhh. No words. No regrets. Come, cara. Let's return to the ship. I am not done making love to you."

His statement hung in the air as Andrea rose and straightened her dress and Lorenzo righted his jeans. Andrea found she wanted nothing more than to be making love with Lorenzo. Oh how this would complicate things now. But damn, the way he looked at her with such a heated gaze once again melted her insides, and she wanted to prolong how she felt at this moment for as long as she could.

He offered her his hand, and once she took it, he yanked her into his embrace, affectionately kissing her again before he hurriedly tugged her after him in his haste to return to the ship.

Chapter Seven

Lorenzo looked down at Andrea, nestled beside him, her face resting against his chest. He didn't remember ever feeling this satisfied or complete. The prospect of spending the entire day making love to her while the ship traveled to Tunisia made him smile. They were good together, that was for sure, but there was always the uncertainty of what would happen once the cruise ended. He also couldn't expect Andrea to leave a job she liked and her life in Chicago and move to Italy. The thought of her near the man who treated her so badly sent a pang of jealously through him. What a predicament they were in, one he was sure was only a step away from heartache. He should have kept quiet about his feelings, never sent the text to her. They could have both gone on with their lives without the conflict this relationship would entail. A part-time love was not an option for Lorenzo. He couldn't give away only half his heart. Damn but he should have thought of this before running back to her. He hadn't considered all the sacrifice required to make this relationship work or the fact that maybe she wouldn't give up the man she was involved with.

Perhaps sleeping with Andrea had happened too fast, both of them being caught up in the moment and the atmosphere. Nevertheless, he had to admit, what incredible sex it was. This night had been amazing, one that could cause a man to rethink all his life plans.

He brushed a lock of hair off her forehead. God, but he would love to wake every morning just like this, with her in his arms all soft and sexy. He hardened with the anticipation of her waking. He would find a way, he told himself, as she turned in his arms, her eyes fluttered open. There had to be a way he could be with her.

"Morning." Her voice was husky with sleep.

He found her half-drowsy state extremely arousing.

"Buon giorno, bella. Did you sleep well?" Lorenzo adored the blush that rose on her cheeks at his question. Of course she'd slept well. She had been so thoroughly ravished by him during the night they had both been near exhaustion by their love play.

He languidly captured her lips, halting any answer that may have been forthcoming. His kiss, while passionate, did not hold the urgency the previous nights had held. Lorenzo wanted to make love unhurriedly, exploring every inch of her body, watching her react to his touch. He wanted to see her nipple pucker when he ran his thumb over it. He wanted to feel her squirm when he buried his fingers inside her warm body and feel her clench around him when she came.

They had nowhere to be today as the ship was en route. The slower paced loving suited this quiet morning just fine. When they got hungry, room service could bring food; when they tired, they could nap. As far as he was concerned, spending the day in bed was the perfect way to pass the time while surrounded by miles of ocean.

Lorenzo trailed kisses down her cheeks, burying his face in the curve of her neck where he kissed the soft skin. He caressed her collarbone and as he did he felt her relax into the bed beneath him.

He tugged down the sheet that covered

her, revealing the rounded tops of her breasts. With his lips, he followed the revealed path, kissing the plump flesh as it was exposed. He moved more of the sheet exposing her peeked nipples, which he took turns lavishing with his tongue. His movements were encouraged by Andrea threading her fingers in his hair, smiling and squealing as he continued playing hide and seek with the sheet and her body.

Inch by inch he kissed and licked every bit of exposed skin. He sought out the junction of her thighs sliding his fingers along the heated flesh, and then slipped them between the swollen folds for more deliberate exploration. Andrea moved against his hand, obviously deriving pleasure from his touch and Lorenzo loved that he was the one who made her squirm.

He continued to kiss her following the same path his fingers had taken. When his tongue reached the tiny nub of her sex, she nearly bucked off the bed. He stroked and coaxed her with his mouth and fingers until he felt her tighten around his hand and come with a very satisfied sigh. Her grateful smile warmed him, and he conveyed his pleasure by kissing her passionately.

Lorenzo was pleased when Andrea sat up and repositioned herself, leaning over him on her elbows. She had a hungry look in her eyes that sent a shiver through him in anticipation of what she was about to do. A moment later, he shamelessly hissed the unexpected breath that caught in his throat as her warm mouth and tongue descended on him, all but rendering him helpless.

She licked, sucked, and stroked him until he was mindless with want of this woman. Several times she brought him to the very brink of losing control and only the thought of her wet and heated body awaiting his entrance gave him a fragment of restraint.

When he finally felt his resistance slipping for the last time, Lorenzo lifted Andrea off him, moving to the edge of the bed. He rolled her to her stomach and positioned himself behind her. With one decisive push, he was inside her and God did she feel good when she clenched around him. He buried himself deep, pulling her back to meet his thrust. He felt the spasms of her orgasm throb around him and that knowledge was all he needed to start him head long into his own climax. He grasped her hips, grinding into her as he came deep inside her.

Morning sex was wonderful, but morning sex with someone you were falling in love with was incredible. The thought made him smile as he gathered her in his arms and laid with her, intent on enjoying every moment of this morning with Andrea.

* * *

Andrea slipped her hand into Lorenzo's as they strolled toward the dining room. Hours of making love had both of them famished and in need of a change of scenery, so together, they decided to temper their passion for a while and have a late lunch, early dinner out in the ship. Although it was still too early for formal dining, the ship boasted a well-stocked buffet always available for those guests who enjoyed less structured dining.

Andrea watch as Lorenzo piled his plate high with food. She couldn't help but smile. He must be starving. Rightly so. He was an incredible lover, tentative and giving. Never had she felt this close to Steve, before, during, or after any time they'd made love. Not so with Lorenzo. There was unspoken warmth between them, evident by looks that passed between them, gentle touches shared, whispered endearments, and ravishing appetites due to the physical activity.

Oh God, she was falling hard for him, and the thought sent warm feelings all the way to her belly. What an unanticipated turn of events. Never had she suspected when receiving tickets for this cruise she'd meet a man who would totally knock her socks off and show her she had nothing with Steve. Now what? Did she admit her feelings to Lorenzo? Oh my, did this just doubly complicate things.

They carried their plates to a small table away from the main dining floor and sat to enjoy their meal.

"You know, I've been thinking of expanding the wine business lately." Lorenzo spoke in between bites of food, looking intently at her. Andrea wondered if he meant into the States. If he opened a business in the States, they could be closer to each other. Things between them could get serious. However, he hadn't said that exactly. So could he be thinking out loud or looking for a reaction from her? Still, she found his statement interesting, especially since she'd thought of nothing but being with him since the previous night.

"It would be great to see your wine in more places except a few exclusive shops."

Lorenzo looked at her with an odd look, so she felt the need to explain further. "It's a little expensive, but you said yourself you have a more modestly priced wine. That would do well."

"How did you learn about my wine?"

"It was through Steve. He might not be much in the romance department, but he is an impeccable wine connoisseur. He travels so much he has the opportunity to try many different kinds. He first introduced me to yours.

Lorenzo nodded in response to her statement, but Andrea got the uncanny feeling he had been thinking of something else as she spoke."

"Andrea, expanding the business would allow me to move to the States. It would allow us to be together, if you still want that."

Andrea froze in mid-movement of taking a bite. He *had* been thinking of something else. He'd been thinking the exact thing as she. She lowered her fork and looked intently at Lorenzo.

"Are you serious? You really want to be with me?"

"Si. That's why I came. That's why I texted you."

That feeling of warmth that had earlier taken root in her stomach spread throughout every part of her. Lorenzo wanted to be with her and she could think of nothing more wonderful than being with him.

"Oh, Lorenzo. I can think of nothing I'd love better."

Lorenzo reached across the table and took her hand. "Anch'io, cara. Me, too."

"And what about Steve?" Lorenzo asked with caution.

"I will talk to him. I've been thinking about our relationship. It's time he and I have a conversation."

"Are you sure?"

"I am sure."

Lorenzo nodded and resumed eating. A moment later, he paused.

"To change the subject, shall we go into Tunisia this evening or wait until tomorrow? Is there anything you want to do or see?" he asked.

"I haven't given it a thought. I don't know anything about this place. I don't have any plans."

"Then why don't we go to the concierge desk after dinner and see what is available to do in port tomorrow," he suggested. "We could catch a show or go dancing on the ship tonight, or just go back to the cabin for our own fun." Lorenzo smiled, raising his brows in a teasing gesture.

"You are wicked."

"Si." Lorenzo reached across the table and squeezed her hand.

"Let's skip the dancing and just go back to

the cabin." Andrea smiled.

"I like that idea best." Lorenzo smirked.

Chapter Eight

Lorenzo stared at the text message on his phone with the same despair he felt the first time he had read it this morning in Andrea's cabin. He just couldn't believe it. His grandfather always seemed such a rock, strong and sturdy. He was shocked to hear his grandfather had collapsed without warning and was in the hospital. He had received the text from his grandmother immediately upon waking.

He had told the old man numerous times he worked too hard, but Nonno refused to hear it. He poured his heart and soul into all aspects of the wine production, from planting the grapes to bottling the wine. The passion his nonno held for the business was extensive, and Lorenzo hoped to share even a part of such incredible dedication, which is why Lorenzo was ready to share their wine with the world. He knew if he could just get the wine into people's hands, the love and dedication of his grandfather would be well received and the quality recognized by the public.

Lorenzo let out a long breath as disappointment overcame him. The idea of expansion would have to wait. Someone now had to run the everyday operations in Italy. Damn but he had just shared an incredibly romantic night with Andrea, making love then talking until the wee hours of the morning about how he planned to bring the business to America. Everything seemed so perfect during the few hours they were together. The future with her seemed as bright and hopeful as the future of the business.

Lorenzo stared out the plane window. A myriad of thoughts churned in his brain. How in just the span of a few hours his life had changed. Last evening he spoke of plans to move to America to be with Andrea. Now, there was no way he could ever leave Italy.

His heart broke. He would not ask Andrea to move, to leave a job and friend she told him she loved. That would be selfish of him and he would not ask her to make that sacrifice. He held no other option but to let her go back to her life. After the initial shock passed, Andrea would see it was for the best. She could return to her life, her job, maybe even Steve, once her vacation was over, and carry on without disruption.

Still, he didn't think he would ever get over the thought of her with a man that treated her with such indifference. He hoped she would still break it off with Steve. He hoped she would find someone that would make her happy, someone that would take her to see Botticelli paintings. He could not swallow the lump forming in his throat as he thought of her gazing on "Primavera."

He was sure it was in that moment he fell in love with her. Her openness, her sincerity touched him deeply. He would remember that day always and tuck it away for when the loneliness hit him in the dark of the night, as he would never forget the image from this morning of her sadly waving good-bye from the ship as he departed.

He closed his eyes for a moment, at the same time the vibration of his phone drew his attention. A text from Andrea.

I hope you made it to the airport and were able to get a flight home. My thoughts are with your grandfather and you. Take care, Lorenzo. Let me know how he is when you can. I miss you.

Lorenzo raised his chin in the air, desperately searching for resolve he didn't feel. He took a deep breath and glanced back down at the message. With false bravado, he hit the delete button and slipped the phone back into his pocket.

Chapter Nine

Andrea hurriedly tossed the last of her belongings in her carryon. She felt a sense of relief that she'd finally heard from Lorenzo in a message delivered to her cabin this morning. She had been so worried about him and his grandfather. He hadn't returned any of her texts or calls since leaving her in Tunisia over two days ago, and then her phone began acting up and she was not able to contact him. She feared the worst had happened with his grandfather. However, as she prepared to depart the ship for the last time, a message arrived stating he would meet her in the departure area. Andrea found it amusing that he once again signed the message "Steve," but then realized he'd never left Steve's paperwork in the cabin and must still have it on him.

The past two days were the longest and

most unbearable she had ever spent. Despite visiting the Bardo Museum in Tunisia and beautiful Catania with its lovely churches, popular fish market, and traditional puppet theater, her mind wasn't on the remainder of her vacation. She spent hours wandering the ship, exploring every shop, theater, restaurant, casino, trying to take her mind off the fact she wasn't able to talk to Lorenzo. No amount of distractions could keep her thoughts from straying back to him. Andrea was more than disheartened that her phone had stopped international calling. She missed talking to Lorenzo. She told herself he would meet her when she docked and she should be patient. She wanted to think the best.

The long hours seemed endless, and as the last two days of her holiday ticked away, she became more and more distraught, thinking she might not get to talk to him before she returned home. She didn't want to leave Italy without seeing him and find out when he thought he might be coming to the States.

An equally distressing idea occurred to her as the previous thought crossed her mind. What if he wasn't coming back? What if he never intended on answering her? What if the whole grandfather thing was just a rouse to give him an escape from her? What if their times together only constituted a brief sex fling? Andrea groaned.

She found these questions settling in the pit of her stomach like a lead shot. His lack of communication would certainly answer those questions. It wouldn't be the first time an unsuspecting American girl fell for the sweet words of a foreign man. But no. She had difficulty believing he would do that to her, especially after showing up so unexpectedly to see her and explaining in detail how he wanted to grow his wine business. She didn't want to believe he could be so cruel and all the things he told her were lies. Still, she'd harbored a nagging feeling of doubt... until she received the message that he would be meeting her. Now she couldn't pack fast enough.

Andrea spied the keychain Lorenzo gave her laying amongst her things on the bed as she packed. Picking it up, she turned it over in her hands remembering when he had given it to her. That afternoon had been one of the best in her life. Thinking back, that was possibly the moment she fell for Lorenzo. His simple gift carried so much thought, so much kindness it warmed her to think about it still. She smiled, tucking the keychain in her pocket before zipping up her bag.

After glancing up and down the hall to

make sure the ship's crew picked up her checked bag, Andrea headed toward the disembarking area, anxious to see Lorenzo. She could hardly stand the wait to check out.

It was to the crew's credit that checkout progressed smoothly and her wait was minimal. Tugging along her carryon, Andrea exited onto the gangway scanning the sea of people gathering, waiting for passengers leaving the ship. She was sure Lorenzo's height and dark hair would be easy to spot. Her heart pounded with excitement. *Boy... this must be love,* she thought laughingly to herself, spying someone she thought might be him, way at the end of the walkway.

"Andrea!"

At first, Andrea didn't hear her name shouted above the din of the crowd. She rose on her tiptoes, trying to see over the disembarking passengers. She walked a ways down the ramp, thinking she might get a better view of the people waiting and wave to Lorenzo if it was in fact him.

"Andrea," came the voice again.

Andrea froze. That wasn't Lorenzo's voice. She recognized that voice. Her stomach instantly churned.

"Hey, Andi." Steve's greeting reached her, and she spun around to see him pushing his way through the crowd toward her, waving, trying to elicit her attention.

"Andrea. Baby. See I did come." Steve grabbed Andrea up into his arms, swinging her around until she was dizzy. When he sat her down, he didn't even give her a second to breath before smashing his lips against hers with a welcoming kiss. He pulled her high into his arms, unbalancing her, and she once again found herself on her tiptoes, this time hanging on to his jacket to keep from falling.

Andrea broke the kiss and pulled back, hiding the disappointment she felt at seeing Steve. She halfheartedly listened to him explain how he arranged his schedule to be able to meet her, all the while she continued searching the crowd over Steve's shoulder for the person she thought might have been Lorenzo.

"Andi, I sent you a message. Didn't you get it?"

Andrea pulled her attention back to Steve. "Huh? What? You sent the note?"

This time she didn't hide her shock. "I'm sorry. Yes. I got it. I'm sorry." The message she thought had been from Lorenzo had actually been from Steve.

"I know. You're surprised to see me. I get it. I surprised myself, coming all this way." Steve continued to talk on, but Andrea didn't hear a word of what he said. She felt her heart sinking to her toes. Lorenzo hadn't sent the note. He wasn't coming to meet her. Sadness instantly gripped her when she realized he wasn't coming. Her heart broke into a million pieces while she tried desperately to hang on to her composure and act as if she couldn't be more thrilled Steve was here. All, the while she was actually dying inside.

"I had my assistant try to make calls to you."

"You did?"

"Something must be messed up with international calling. We'll figure it out when we get home. You won't need it anyway, right?" He squeezed her hand and smiled down at her.

"Right." She nodded, putting on a false smile that once again belied her true feelings. She one last time searched the faces of the people around her in a last ditch attempt to find Lorenzo. Nevertheless, hope was irrevocable dashed when she accepted he wasn't there.

"Andi? Andrea? Are you ready to go? I've got a taxi waiting."

"Huh? Yes."

"Are you all right?"

No, she wasn't all right. "Yes, I'm just tired. It's been a long trip."

"Well, let's get you to the airport. We'll grab a bite to eat there."

Steve reached for her hand, instead of the suitcase, she noted, and tugged her down the gangway ramp toward the waiting taxi, her heart breaking in two as she walked.

She wasn't half way down the ramp when she heard her name called and once again, it took a moment for it to register, being so lost in her thoughts.

"Andrea...! Signorina Andrea McDonald."

Andrea turned in the direction of the voice to find the young cherub-faced crewmember, running down the gangplank in her direction waving a slip of paper, his blond curls bobbing as he ran.

Andrea stopped, yanking her hand away from Steve who stopped a few steps farther down, impatiently stomping his foot as he waited.

"Signorina...." came the crewman's huffed greeting, as he halted in front of Andrea and caught his breath. He straightened his jacket, making himself presentable after his little dash. "I'm glad I caught you." He smiled a wide smile as he looked at her.

"What's the matter, Mr. Cupido?"

"This came for you earlier; however, you'd already left. I was afraid I wouldn't find you to give it to you."

Andrea noticed that as he handed her the slip of paper, Mr. Cupido raised his gaze to Steve and scrunched his eyes. She thought it must be the sun and shifted to her right to help block it.

Andrea looked down at the slip of paper in her hands as a strange feeling came over her. She knew this moment was one of those moments that marked a person's life. She didn't know why, but sensed it just the same. She found it odd that she recognized it and knew if she opened the envelope something would change. She paused, afraid of what would happen.

The crewman gently touched her arm. "Open it, Signorina." He spoke softly, only for her to hear.

Andrea looked up at him then back down at the slip of paper. Drawing a deep breath, she unfolded the message.

I will meet you at the dock. L. aka Steve.

Andrea stared at the note for what seemed ages while she digested what the message meant. It meant Lorenzo *had* come for her. It meant that the person she thought she saw several minutes ago could have been him and he was here or *was* here. Maybe she was right in her assumption he couldn't have contacted her until now.

Andrea looked back up at Mr. Cupido, not hiding the confusion and surprise she felt. Yes, this was one of those moments, she noted, looking at the grinning young man, one of those moments where an instant decision would change one's path in life forever.

Andrea looked over at Steve who didn't hide his annoyance at the interruption to their departure. She turned back to the young crewman.

"Go to him," the young man whispered. "Go after him."

Andrea needed no other coaxing than those simple words to know exactly what her heart wanted to do. She threw her arms around the startled crewmember hugging him.

"Thank you. Thank you so much for bringing me this."

"Non e niente, bella. Now go." He chuckled, pleased with himself.

Without further hesitation, she grabbed her travel bag and brushed past Steve, running down the gangway ramp.

"Hey!" Steve shouted.

"I'm sorry!" she called back over her shoulder before disappearing from sight.

Chapter Ten

Lorenzo pushed the cork back into the testing cask and set down the glass of wine he'd pulled to taste. Good. *The best yet,* he thought, patting the keg as if it were a child who had done a good deed. At least something was right. Lorenzo turned to leave the fermenting area, running smack into the very person he was on his way to see.

"You are back from the docks? So soon?"

"Si. You're supposed to be resting, Nonno."

His grandfather waved his hands. "Nonsenso. I'm tired of resting. There is too much to do." His grandfather picked up the half-full glass Lorenzo had tasted and took a drink of the wine, savoring the flavor in his mouth for several seconds.

"Meraviglioso!" he stated, pleased with

what he tasted.

"I'm glad you approve, Nonno."

"Si."

Lorenzo lifted the glass from his grandfather's hands and took the old man's elbow, leading him out of the dark room and into another part of the brewing building.

"Come, I will walk you back to the house. You need to regain your strength. The doctor said you need to take it easy."

"I will slow down when I die." His grandfather protested, stubbornly pulling his arm away from Lorenzo. He gazed on his grandson with concern etching his expression.

"I will go rest, si, but not until you tell me why you returned without her and why you hide out here."

"It is a long story, Nonno. She won't be coming."

Lorenzo's grandfather gave him a look that told Lorenzo he wouldn't pursue the reason for now. Instead, the old man patted Lorenzo's arm and turned, leaving Lorenzo alone.

Lorenzo sighed. He felt like he had died all over again this morning. Once again left alone by someone he dared give his heart.

Lorenzo knew his plans for moving to the States had vanished once his grandfather took ill. He wanted so badly to ask Andrea to move to Italy with him, yet previous experience with his fiancé kept him silent. After several unsuccessful attempts to reach her by phone, his grandfather convinced him to go to her this morning, take the chance, and ask her to come to Italy.

Lorenzo ran his hand through his hair. He would never know if she would've said yes. He hadn't stuck around to ask. She appeared pleased to be meeting Steve, and Lorenzo hadn't wanted to spoil the happy reunion. He also hadn't wanted to deal with dejection a second time. Therefore, he'd left. All hopes and possibilities had left with him, which was why he was here, pining away for what would never be. He let his fear cloud his judgment. He should have just gone to her, given her the choice. Instead, he walked away, feigning indifference to salvage, his wounded pride at seeing her with someone else.

Lorenzo punched one of the wine vats in frustration, his action only serving to bruise his knuckles. Damn his fiancé, damn his lack of courage. Lorenzo stormed out of the building, climbed onto one of the ATVs, and sped away toward the fields.

* * *

Andrea climbed the stone stairs of the old villa house and crossed the porch, apprehension filling her at what she might find. A door was open, but she heard no noise coming from the inside the home. She was positive she was at the right place, because the sign at the entrance proudly announced the name of the vineyard. Still, she was nervous.

She knocked on the wooden framed screen door.

"Hello?" she called. "Is anyone home?"

She knocked again. "Ciao? C'è qualcuno in casa?"

She heard nothing in response to her call, and turned to look out over the gently rolling hills of the surrounding land. Way out against the horizon she saw a plume of dirt indicating a vehicle moved about; however, the distance wasn't feasible for her to try to reach on foot. There were several buildings scattered around the premises she supposed she could try. Andrea drew a deep breath. The vineyard was beautiful. No wonder Lorenzo loved it so much. It was full of old world charm and warmth.

"Caio."

A voice came from the house, startling Andrea. She spun around to find an older gentleman opening the door.

"Caio."

"Excuse my Italian, er, chiedo scusa per il mio Italiano. I'm looking for Lorenzo. Sto cercando Lorenzo."

A grateful laugh greeted her attempt at Italian. "I speak English, cara." The older man spoke.

Andrea huffed, relieved. "Oh."

"You are the American from the ship, no?"

"Si... I mean yes."

The gentleman opened the door wider, inviting Andrea inside.

"Are you Lorenzo's grandfather?"

"Si. Niccolo."

Andrea smiled, relieved. "I am so glad you are well, Niccolo." She sincerely meant that. He graced her with a smile that said he appreciated her concern.

She followed Niccolo down a hallway adorned with framed scenes from Roman mythology. Venus, Bacchus, and Cupid, were just a few characters she recognized in the old paintings. After a few more steps, she found herself entering a spacious kitchen, where Niccolo motioned for her to have a seat at the rustic table.

"Would you like something to drink? Wine? Tea?"

Andrea thought for a moment. The situation she found herself in called for something stronger than tea, something that would calm her nerves and give her the courage to confront Lorenzo.

"Wine," she replied after a few moments.

Niccolo brought two glasses and a bottle of red wine over to table. He poured a glass and passed it over to her. He poured a second for himself and sat with her.

"Salute." Andrea raised her glass, toasting to Niccolo.

"Salute, cara."

While Niccolo only sipped his glass, Andrea downed the contents of hers in one long drink. Niccolo instantly refilled her glass.

"So you are here to see my Lorenzo?"

"Yes."

"Lorenzo said you have an American boyfriend."

"No. Not anymore."

"Good. From what I heard, he was not good."

"No, he wasn't," Andrea agreed.

"You like my Lorenzo?"

"Very much, but I'm not sure what our future holds. That's what I came to find out."

"Lorenzo has a noble heart if not misguided."

"I don't know what to think about what happened between us. One minute he talked about plans to move to the States, the next minute he was gone."

"I do know that Lorenzo cares deeply for you."

"I don't understand what happened."

Niccolo drank the contents of his glass, and poured himself a refill, all the while looking like he formed his thoughts.

"Cara, did Lorenzo tell you about his fiancé?"

"He told me that she left him at the church on the day of their wedding."

"Did he tell you why?"

"He said because she secretly loved another."

"Well, that is only partly true."

"Oh?" Andrea took a sip of her wine.

"His fiancé harbored lot of anger about leaving her home, friends, and family and moving to Italy with him. She never told him that she didn't want to do this. She led him to believe it was what she wanted. Her true feelings festered underneath their relationship and in secret caused a lot of resentment on her part. Not once did she ever mention her love for her home or job. She spoke only as if leaving was acceptable to her. She never told him she didn't want to come to Italy."

Niccolo took a drink of his wine.

"Lorenzo isn't innocent in all this, mind you," he began. "Because the two of them should have discussed this and didn't. But had he even a small idea she didn't want to leave, he would have never asked her to move."

"That explains why Lorenzo wanted to come to the States to expand the business. He wanted us to be together, but he wouldn't ask me to give up my life."

"Exactly, cara. When I got sick, Lorenzo knew he couldn't move to America and would never ask you to abandon your career and friends and move to Italy. So he chose to allow you to return home to your life."

"That's rather presumptuous."

"And I told him that. I reminded him he would never know if he didn't ask, so I sent him back to the ship early this morning."

Andrea fished in her purse and pulled out the message she'd received from the crewmember as she had departed. "I didn't get his message until I was already checked out and halfway down the gangway." She passed over the letter to Niccolo who read it.

"I did receive one from Steve earlier that morning that I thought was from Lorenzo."

"I see." Niccolo spoke, setting down the letter.

"My heart was broken when I found Steve

instead of Lorenzo there to meet me. I thought Lorenzo abandoned me. I didn't know Lorenzo had been there. I didn't know."

Andrea set down her glass she had been twirling in her fingers. "I need to talk to him."

"Well, Cara, I know where he is."

* * *

Andrea hung onto Niccolo's jacket for dear life as the older man maneuvered the ATV over the bumpy terrain. The jostling of the vehicle as they made their way through the vineyard made her regret the wine she'd drunk. She hoped she didn't embarrass herself by getting ill.

Just when she thought she'd reached her tolerance, she felt the vehicle slow, then come to a stop. She peered around Niccolo's shoulders and saw Lorenzo busily pruning a grapevine, unaware of her presence. Niccolo climbed off the ATV.

"Nonno, I thought you were supposed to rest...." Lorenzo chastised his grandfather without even looking up.

Andrea slid off the vehicle and stood next to Niccolo. "It's my fault."

Andrea watched as Lorenzo raised his head. A stunned expression crossed his face while his eyes revealed a myriad of uncertainties.

Andrea stepped forward. "I didn't know you came."

"It didn't look like it mattered much." Lorenzo's voice held bitterness as he snipped at a vine.

"It mattered. I thought you were meeting me. I didn't know it would be Steve."

The sound of Niccolo's ATV roaring away interrupted further conversation until the noise died down. Lorenzo stood and stepped to his vehicle, setting down his pruning shears.

"You kissed him."

"He grabbed me before I knew it." I was in shock he wasn't you."

"Andrea...."

"Why didn't you contact me?"

"I tried, your service was disconnected. I thought you disconnected it."

"Oh." Andrea, remembered Steve saying he had tried to contact her, also.

"I thought I'd meet you at the dock, but then I saw you with him."

"I looked for you. I even thought I saw you. Then Steve arrived. I didn't get your message until we were nearly off the dock."

Andrea twirled her toe in the dirt while she waited for Lorenzo to speak, but he didn't.

She recalled what his grandfather told her moments before and decided the only way to clear the air was to take it upon herself to do so.

"I don't want to be with Steve. I want to be with you." Lorenzo looked at her then and she could swear she saw his resolve crumble at that second.

"And how does he feel about this?"

"I don't know. I just left him there. On the gangway."

"Really?"

Andrea laughed, realizing she'd left Steve the way he'd left her.

"Oh my."

Lorenzo took one step forward and pulled her against him, abruptly stifling any remaining words Andrea was going to say. His lips hovered above hers.

"So I guess I should ask... will you come live with me?" he breathed, a hairbreadth from kissing her.

The single word she replied fell away as his mouth covered hers in a scorching kiss that would make the ancient God's proud...

... and they were.

Finito
The End

ABOUT THE AUTHOR

Angela Aaron's love affair with writing began at nine years old when inspired by the "will they ever be together" relationship between Candy and Jeremy on "Here Comes The Brides." She filled notebook after notebook of "happily-ever-afters" for these characters. She hasn't stopped writing since. Angie's true love has always been romance and erotic romance with lots of sizzling moments between her characters and a happily ever after ending.

Angie is from the Midwest. She is a mother, works full time, and includes her rescued Bouviers and Poodle as part of the family. Angie is extremely down to earth, and hates phony people. Angie has to be outdoors as much as possible and finds her inspiration from the lakes and forests which surround her. She hates winter, loves summer and sun. She loves the moon and night time. She is an "autumn." She loves chocolate, a good romance and bag pipe music. She is completely at home in the water. She loves fantasy and believes in magic.

Pleasure Island was first released in 2011, with the second edition re-released in 2013. Angie's second book, **The Fire of Beltane** was released in 2012, with the re-release in 2013.

For more info on Angela Aaron please visit her web page: http://angelaaaronauthor.yolasite.com/ or find her on Facebook.